DETERMINED IS HER PATH

SCHOOL OF NECESSARY MAGIC™ BOOK SEVEN

JUDITH BERENS   MARTHA CARR   MICHAEL ANDERLE

L M B P N

DISRUPTIVE IMAGINATION

Thanks to Early Readers

Debi Sateren
Michael Robbins
Kathleen Fettig
Terry Hicks Bennett
Bep Hvilsted-Koopman

Thanks to the JIT Readers

Misty Roa
Danika Fedeli
Keith Verret
Angel LaVey
Daniel Weigert
Nicole Emens
Larry Omas
Paul Westman

If we've missed anyone, please let us know!

DEDICATIONS

From Martha

To everyone who still believes in magic
and all the possibilities that holds.
To all the readers who make this
entire ride so much fun.
And to my son, Louie and so many wonderful friends who
remind me all the time of what
really matters and how wonderful
life can be in any given moment.

From Michael

To Family, Friends and
Those Who Love
To Read.
May We All Enjoy Grace
To Live The Life We Are
Called.

CHAPTER ONE

The polished, red train car pulled away in a cloud of steam, picking up speed until it disappeared in a fast swish headed to the next stop. The platform was full of commuters brushing past Alison Brownstone. She adjusted the magical glasses, still amazed at seeing everything. She grabbed the handle on her suitcase and headed for the first set of long, crisscrossed stairs to the top.

A swirl of magic caught Alison's attention drawing her from her thoughts. Thick crimson lines cut through the shadow cast by the low ceiling over the underground railroad platform. She tensed and slowly looked around for the culprit. A young girl dressed in purple pants and a white down vest was filled with worried pink soul energy and scatterings of anxious greys. She stood near the edge of the platform, whispering as she cast a spell. Upon closer inspection, Alison saw the magic didn't have any malice within it, but that didn't change the fact it was illegal and needed to be stopped before the authorities noticed.

She strode over to the girl who hurriedly stopped her spell and stilled her hands when she saw Alison.

"You should be careful, casting magic here is illegal." Alison looked around to make sure no one else had seen.

The younger girl's eyes widened upon hearing the word illegal.

"I was just trying to see if I'm in the right place." The younger girl shifted her weight, refusing to meet Alison's eyes.

Alison looked at her and the suitcase by her side. "Are you by any chance going to the School of Necessary Magic?"

The girl relaxed, and her soul energies slowly turned a calm, pale blue with flecks of gold excitement.

"I'm Christie Bealls, a witch, you know." She tapped the wand in her hand. "I've never been this far from home before. I'm a transfer student, and it took me the entire summer break to convince my dad not to ride the train with me. Overprotective wizard, you know. He gave me the wand he had when he went to Marlborough College. Made of Chestnut!" She had a distinctive British accent and kept tucking a dark brown curl behind her ear. Everything came out in a flood of words.

"Wow, that's a lot of info all at once. My name is Alison Brownstone." She put out her hand, and Christie grasped it, giving a vigorous shake. Alison saw the dove tattoo on her wrist.

"I get it. I was new once too, seems like yesterday. Don't worry. Soon, the school will feel like a home away from home. Come on. Let's head up to Starbucks."

Christie relaxed and fell into step alongside Alison.

They had almost reached the stairs when she could no longer bear the quiet.

"You really do go to the school, right?"

Alison smiled. "Your *first* time ever traveling alone? Yes, I'll be starting my senior year there. How about we take the jitney together? You're from England?"

They began their ascent of the winding stairs up toward Starbucks. Small groups of other students were chatting about their summer adventures as they made their way up to the coffee shop, and the jitney that would arrive there in a while.

"London. This is my first time in America."

Christie's gaze bounced back and forth between other groups of students, the commuters, and Alison. Alison watched the excitement bloom within the girl forming soft ribbons of gold against the pale blue of her soul energy.

"I've never seen London. What's it like?"

She led Christie around the next bend of the stairs, stepping back to let a crush of travelers heading across to another set of stairs marked *Europe, Express*.

They needed to cross back and forth several times before reaching the exit into the Starbucks at the top. The railroad was hidden from humans and provided quick transport for magicals to any destination in the world.

"Very different to this!" Christie laughed. "London is very grey and heavy. It can feel as if the city is closing in on you sometimes. The parks are nice, but they feel too manicured. I heard the school was set on huge grounds. I can't wait to be surrounded by greenery. London's okay, I guess. It's like a micro-country."

Alison smiled, listening to the stream of words. She

gestured for Christie to turn right and begin climbing the last flight of stairs.

"How so?"

Christie frowned and chewed her bottom lip. "Well, each part of London has a different feel to it. And there are lots of different accents. I don't know, forget I said anything. Is it true there was a big battle against dark forces?"

Alison's step faltered for half a beat.

"Yes. Yes, that's true. Don't worry about that though, which class are you most excited to be taking?"

"This will sound really dorky… but I'm looking forward to the history of Oriceran. I mean, it's fascinating, don't you think? And we can learn so much from history. I know I'm supposed to say casting or something, but I think history's cool. I've read everything there is on the Silver Griffins. Boy, I wish they still existed. Can you imagine going out there to fight against evil?"

Alison walked right through the wall into the Starbucks, coming out by the bathrooms. The glamour worked, and the one human heading toward the men's room didn't even look at her.

The exits in every Starbucks were hidden in a large alcove near the bathrooms where there was a glamour making all of it invisible to any human coming down the short hall. Once Christie had joined her, they stepped out into the main room as if they'd just left the bathroom.

"History's important. Knowing where we come from is a key part of understanding who and what we are. Can I ask, how old are you?"

"Oh, did I leave that out? I'm thirteen and a half. I

finished middle school early. The teachers said I was beyond their capabilities. Not exactly sure what they meant by that, but there was a meeting, and everyone decided I'd be better off starting high school early. Something about teaching me how to use my wand more effectively, you know?"

Alison gave her a sideways glance, watching the swirl of colors inside of Christie. "You're in the right place."

Christie beamed at her as they made their way between the wide, comfortable chairs where human students from UVA were sitting with townies and magicals from the School of Necessary Magic. All of them were lounging around small round tables. Familiar acoustic music from that day's featured musician played from the speakers, adding to the comfortable, relaxed vibe.

Alison scanned the energies of the people around her looking for familiar faces but didn't see anyone. Things just weren't the same without Izzie. It was the first time she wasn't greeted by her at the train platform since she had started the school. She shook her head. *Maybe I'll get a message from her soon.*

"Grande gingerbread latte with extra cream please," Christie ordered, as she played with the tag on her bag.

"Tall latte, please," Alison ordered, gently putting her hand on the other girl's upper arm.

"You're going to be fine. Think of it as the beginning of an epic adventure."

"Epic adventure," she whispered, the smile growing on her face. "With a wand!"

"Little quieter in town." Alison smiled at the human

standing behind her. Almost no one in town knew the school was full of magicals, not yet anyway.

Christie nodded, not saying another word. "I didn't mean you couldn't speak at all."

They paid the barista and Alison moved down to wait by the end of the counter where she looked around the large room for an open table.

The barista handed them their lattes, and they made their way to a quiet table in the corner with a clear view of the sidewalk outside.

"Did you do much over the summer?"

Alison settled herself into her chair and thought for a moment. Shay and Brownstone had gotten married, but she wasn't sure how to explain that to Christie. *That's a complicated story. Maybe save that one for the girl's second day.* It had been a simple, classy affair. The couple had looked happy. Their souls glowed with love and happiness for weeks afterwards.

"I did a lot of work with my magic with Shay; she's kind of my mom. Trained with her on an obstacle course. I'm thinking about becoming a bounty hunter like my dad. What about you?"

"I went to a few concerts, but mostly my parents had me studying so I would stay out of trouble." Christie gave a nervous laugh, tucking a curl behind her ear as she chewed on her bottom lip.

"I haven't really come into my magic yet. Mum's worried that I might not know what I'm doing if I have to actually use magic some day. She thinks I spend too much time hiding and reading when I should be out there playing sports and refining my magic. Truth is, I found a cache of old spell books they had buried that belonged to ancient Bealls. I've been practicing all summer. Only burned a pillow, and boy, those things go up fast. Whoosh!" She threw up her hands, rolling her eyes. "And, okay broke that window, but I fixed that with the old wand before anyone saw, so that doesn't really count. Frankly, shows I learned a thing or two, so it's a win-win. I'm pretty sure Mom's hoping I'll find a nice boyfriend too."

Alison had to laugh. The girl could talk without taking a breath and seemed to have no filters. "I'm sure plenty of guys will be more than happy to fill that role."

Christie blushed, and her energies took on an embarrassed hue. Alison reached across the table and squeezed her hand.

"There's no rush to do anything. The world needs magical bookworms just as much as they need jocks."

"Or badass bounty hunters."

"Yeah, or badass bounty hunters."

They finished up their lattes and walked outside into the warm fall day. The humidity had dropped to bearable levels, and the leaves were beginning to change different colors in the Blue Ridge mountains. The air buzzed with excitement and nerves as students gathered outside the Starbucks, waiting for Mrs. Beasley and the jitney. Christie remained close to Alison, playing with the tag on her bag and looking around her. "I just don't want to miss a thing. This is the first day of my new adventure."

The smaller bus pulled up exactly on time, and the students jostled and pushed their way forward vying to get their preferred seats.

"Find a seat. There's room for everyone," Mrs. Beasley

cheerily called, grunting as she shoved the handle, closing the door.

Alison and Christie sat near the back in a comfortable silence while the few stragglers tried to find seats. A couple of junior boys Alison recognized, sat in the row opposite the girls and pulled out their wands, giving each other a knowing look. Alison rolled her eyes when she saw the familiar glow of magic form in the tip of their wands before small orbs of light began bouncing around the back of the bus. A young student squeaked in surprise when the light collided with her cheek until a sophomore reached across the aisle and caught the orbs in her hand. She crushed them, leaving nothing but dust.

"No magic on the bus, or else you'll be walking!" Mrs. Beasley shouted, glaring into the rear-view mirror.

Everyone fell silent until the bus began moving, and the conversation started flowing again.

"Do you think they've finished repairing the house yet?"

"Is she a senior? I heard she was involved in the big fight last year."

"What about dark forces?"

Alison shut it all out and tried to focus on the year ahead. She'd be seeing her friends and Tanner again soon. No Izzie, but it had to be that way.

CHAPTER TWO

Alison got off the bus and looked around for Emma and Kathleen, or maybe Aya.

Tanner's familiar smile caught her eye over by the large, wrought iron gates that marked the entrance to the school grounds. Christie had already vanished in the crowd and was being pulled along by a pair of pretty, raven-haired girls who were assigned to show around new students.

Groups of students, new and old were saying goodbye to their parents and guardians up by the circular driveway. Alison made her way around a pair of what looked to be freshmen girls as their mother chided them. "Make sure you mind the professors." The girls rolled their eyes. "Yes, mother."

Older students waved their parents off and strode onto the grounds without so much as a backward glance.

Tanner casually leaned against the gate waiting for Alison to reach him, smiling. A few of the younger girls looked at the handsome senior and nudged each other, not that he noticed. He only had eyes for Alison. The orphaned wizard's soul energies pulsed with soft roses and pale lilacs, showing his deep affections for Alison. He pushed off the gate and greeted his girlfriend with a broad grin as he wrapped his arms around her waist.

"I missed you," he said before he kissed her with a deep longing that had filled him throughout the summer.

Alison enjoyed the blissful moment where the world slipped away, leaving nothing but the contentment at being back in his arms.

"Move along!" an older woman shouted as she glared at the couple and ushered them inside the gates.

Tanner held Alison close with his arm around her waist. He didn't miss the way she tensed as she looked over the mansion. The renovations were mostly completed, but the building still bore the scars of the huge fight against the dark magicals. The east wing was bare and exposed where workers were busily plastering the new brick under Horace's watchful eye. The flame-red hair of the groundskeeper stood out against the rolling emerald green lawns like a beacon.

Both teenagers stood a little taller and set their shoulders back as they approached, the memories of the blood and loss washing away the happiness at seeing each other. It had only hardened Alison's resolve to follow in Brownstone's footsteps and become a bounty hunter. She was going to fight to make the world a safer place. Tanner kissed her temple. "Do anything fun over the summer?"

They walked around a huddle of juniors who were talking about Mr. Hodges.

"He's hot, and he's a shifter. I'm sure I could convince him to bend the rules."

"Exactly, he's a shifter. Besides, you could be expelled!"

"Worth it."

"Shay helped me with my magic, and she took me out to train with her on an obstacle course. It was brutal, but I feel like I'm ready, you know?"

Tanner frowned and rubbed his thumb over Alison's hip.

"You know I'll be right there at your side."

In their minds, it wasn't a matter of *if* the dark magicals returned. It was when. The dark families were too determined to claim the power and the place in society that they felt they were owed. Alison wasn't going to let that happen. She would fight with everything she had to keep the people around her safe. She glanced up at Tanner, and her expression softened. He had fought with her and proven himself a skilled and brave warrior. Brownstone would have been proud if he could get past Tanner's gender and see how happy he made his daughter.

"What about you? Do much over summer?"

"I've been practicing a lot with my magic. I found this cool little cabin deep in the woods where I didn't have to worry about anyone seeing. I've nailed this awesome fireball spell, and I'm making progress on a small fire tornado. I tried summoning a badass sword, but it keeps coming out as this little switchblade, which isn't going to do much good. I'll get it though. I think I keep losing focus right near the end. Summoning like that isn't quite as natural as the elements. Have you seen Peter yet?"

They had been casually strolling up the driveway letting the large group of younger students push past them in their eagerness.

"Hey! Wait up!" a familiar male voice called.

Peter and Kathleen jogged behind them while Emma sauntered at her own pace.

"How've you been? How was summer?" Peter asked.

Tanner raised an eyebrow and looked down at the silver suitcase walking by the guy's side.

"I think you should tell us." Tanner smirked.

"Dude, I've been experimenting. Check it out!"

He made a small hand gesture at the suitcase, curling in his fingers. The suitcase skittered in front of him and proceeded to out a small compartment in the top slowly.

Alison peered inside to see six silver and black swirled orbs. Vibrant blue and yellow magic clung to the edge of the orbs like a thin armor laying in even plates.

Peter reached in and picked up an orb before he closed his eyes and pressed his own royal purple magic into the orb. Alison watched raptly as the magical plates slid apart, and delicate blades slowly emerged. To Tanner's eyes, it looked like a deadly translucent shuriken.

"They'll slice through anything from dragon hide to actual armor," Peter said with pride.

"That is badass," Tanner said as he slowly reached out to touch the shuriken.

It had cut through his skin, drawing garnet droplets of blood before he'd even felt the contact. The blood was absorbed into the glass-looking material, and Alison watched as the yellow magic took on a more ochre hue.

"They feed on blood, so they get bigger and sharper."

"And here I was happy that I'd managed to master the four-minute mile and improved my hand-to-hand combat," Emma said wryly.

"Stop dawdling!" Mara called over to them just as Emma finally reached them.

They gave the headmistress apologetic looks and headed toward the house with Emma walked with the group.

"I had the best summer. I met the most *talented* shifter if you know what I mean. I went to three concerts, and I got a brand-new wand made from rosewood," she said, pulling out a long, slender wand made from rich, dark brown wood with golden-chestnut grain.

"So, it's expensive. The real question is, can you use it?" Peter asked.

Emma smiled, and she wasted no time in calling her magic with her new prize.

"Emma, you know better! Put that wand away and make your way inside, now!" Mara called.

"She seems to be in a particularly bad mood," Kathleen said, putting her arm around Emma, as she quickly slid the wand into her pocket.

Alison thought of Izzie and hoped their friend was okay out in the world. She'd been close to the headmistress, who turned out to be her great-grandmother. It must have been hard on Mara Berens.

"What on Earth is *that?*" Kathleen asked Peter as his suitcase stumbled next to him.

"Why carry it when it can walk?"

"Normal people have rolling luggage."

"I have to admit I'd be worried it wouldn't give up my stuff," Emma said.

Peter shook his head and sighed.

"The future is in the mixing of science and magic. Both

can become something so much more when they're combined. Sure, they're cool by themselves but think of the possibilities!"

The conversation died when they reached the old manor and saw the remnants of the damage up close. Alison saw the small gaps in the school's protection spells where the workers were still working. The usual overlays of colorful threads and symbols were dulled, and it only added to the weight of the memories of what had happened, and everything they had lost.

Horace stood on the lawn with his arms crossed and a tight frown on his face. His aunt Estelle was shaking her head again almost losing the cigarette hanging from her painted lips. Her red mane was teased into a high bouffant, which easily added six inches onto her small frame.

"They need to be pushed, Horace. The kids are here now. They should have finished that corner yesterday, and here they are," she said with a thick Texas drawl.

"Things need to be done right."

"I completely agree," Turner Underwood said as he joined them.

Horace dipped his chin a little with respect to the retired Fixer. His white hair was cut in a fashionable if slightly long cut, but it was his navy-blue silk jacket that caught Horace's eye. It wasn't the sort of thing normally seen around the school.

"Well, fill me in," the elf said.

"As you can see, the destroyed windows have been

replaced, and the roof is mostly repaired." Horace gestured to the neat rows of rectangular windows and dark, Welsh slate roof. It had taken them three hours to stop the smoldering of the exposed trusses, but thankfully, they were mostly salvageable. They had engraved the thick, pale oak with new layers of spells to help strengthen the overall protection and safety of the school.

Horace began walking around the west wing where more workers were plastering around a wide door leading into a small kitchen.

"They have been layering spells as they work which has slowed everything down. Wards and magic are now woven into the very fibers and brickwork of the building, and the glass has been reinforced to withstand attacks from magical and human weapons better."

The light elf pursed his lips and sighed softly. The small etchings into the pale plaster around the black door took away some of the simple elegance he had loved about the building. It was necessary of course, but it was another reminder that this wasn't the safe haven he had hoped.

"And the grounds?"

"Horace has fixed those right up," Estelle said.

"Show me."

Horace led the elf over the extensive lawns and gently rolling hills with stunning views of the thick forests covering the Blue Ridge mountains. Where there had been craters and ashy remnants of trees now stood slender trees with gold and amber leaves. Thick, soft grass covered the dark soil that had filled the crater, removing any signs of what had happened there.

The elderly magical nodded his appreciation, and

Horace's chest swelled with pride. He'd worked hard to bring the place back to its full grandeur.

———

Mara closed the door to her office and turned to face Xander. The conversation had been a long time coming. They had confronted each other before but nothing was settled and then Izzie left, leaving an empty space between them. *We need to talk.*

She leaned back against her desk, crossed her arms and steeled herself. She still cared about the man before her. He had been everything she wanted and needed in a man. He was charismatic, dangerous, and head-turning handsome.

"Why did you do it, Mara?"

She squeezed her eyes closed for a moment, trying to ignore the pain in her ex's voice. He was just a friend and professor now.

"I did what was best for Izzie and her parents."

"You said that before Izzie went on the run again."

Her chest tightened at the thought of them on the run. She had tried to keep them safe, but in the end, she had failed.

"You could have told me who she is."

He took a step closer to her, and she lifted her chin not willing to back down.

"I'm sorry, Xander, but Izzie was my priority, and you knowing would not have helped her."

"You wiped her memories! You took away her knowledge of her family."

"Leira and Correk asked me to, and that kept her safe for a few precious years," she said coolly.

"She is my great-granddaughter, I had a right to know!"

"And what would you have done?"

"You forget just what I'm capable of Mara," he ground out.

She knew all too well what he was capable of and the darkness within him.

He calmed himself and picked up a thick, leather-bound book sitting on the edge of her desk. He was close enough to touch. His scent of cloves and fresh earth brought back happy memories of the times they'd enjoyed together. They had been wild and passionate, but it had to end.

"I have many forms of magic at my fingertips. I could have kept her safe. I could have trained her and really shown her how to harness her magic. You hindered her." His eyes met hers, cold and dangerous.

Mara stood and stepped into his personal space.

"I do not regret what I did, Xander. I would do it all again, never doubt that."

He flinched at her words.

"I have not lost the war. I will not lose myself to the darkness," he said softly.

Mara looked away, unwilling to engage.

Xander placed the book back on the desk and left Mara to her own thoughts in the all too quiet office. Izzie meant the world to her, and she would never knowingly put her in harm's way.

CHAPTER THREE

E veryone decided that they needed to start senior year with some fun. A game of dodgeball was the perfect way to clear out the cobwebs and get their minds focused. Alison found herself being distracted by the bold print on a teacher's shirt, and the portrait of Turner Underwood looking regal.

"Come on. He's not even good looking," Kathleen said as she hooked her arm around her friend's and pulled her toward the gym.

They turned a corner and found themselves caught in a bottleneck where scaffolding from the renovations narrowed the usually wide hallway. Students and teachers came through in small groups taking turns to pass. Alison saw the glistening magic of fresh wards being carefully woven into the new plasterwork covering the solid brick. Somehow, it didn't reassure her.

"So, have you and Tanner had some alone time yet? You must be dying to get your hands on him."

Alison's cheeks started to turn pink. She wasn't entirely

comfortable talking about such details even with her closest friends.

They arrived in the spacious gym with well-worn, wooden floors and off-white walls. A group of twenty or so girls spread out throughout the space, talking and laughing as the sunlight started to peek through the narrow windows at the top of the tall walls.

"Quick reminder! The rules are simple. There are no teams. We'll enchant the dodgeball, and whoever can hold onto it for five full seconds wins. If it strikes you, you're out," a peppy young teacher with spiked blonde hair said.

Someone complained about morning people, making Alison smile.

The teacher held onto the large, red rubber ball and pushed burgundy magic into it. Alison watched as the burgundy slowly swelled within the ball and formed a large star shape. The teacher struggled to hold onto it as she finished imbuing it with the last bits of magic.

"Ready? Begin!" she shouted as she released the ball.

Unlike a regular dodgeball that needed to be bounced and thrown, this one had a mind of its own. The girls scattered around the room and watched the ball warily as it bounced in place for a few seconds before it shot off toward a tall brunette girl with broad shoulders and violet sneakers.

The girl dipped into a fighting pose and glared at the ball, daring it to try and strike her. She lunged forward to grab onto it, but it twisted in mid-air and bounced away at the last second. If Alison didn't know better, she'd have sworn it was mocking them.

The ball's magic took on a navy blue hue before it

bounced high then shot downward as a petite green-haired girl looked up alarmed. She moved too slowly, and the ball collided with her chest, sending her flying with a groan of pain.

Alison started moving around the gym in a simple spiral, watching the ball as she tried to figure out its patterns. It bounced away after it struck the green-haired girl, the sounds in an even rhythm like a laugh. She saw it turn navy once more just as it turned and started moving toward Kathleen.

Kathleen wasn't going to be caught unawares. She had a determined look on her face as she side-stepped just as the ball reached her. She grabbed onto the ball and held on with all she had, her face contorting as the ball bucked and slowly began to rise. Kathleen's feet were barely touching the ground when she finally released the ball, and its magic returned to burgundy.

The ball did what could only be described as a victory lap before it took out a pair of slender twins in one fell swoop. Alison was finding it harder to focus with the new glasses. Her vision was torn between the familiar magic and soul energy, and the solid forms of her classmates.

Another girl tried to grasp the ball only to be dragged a few feet before she lost her grip on it. Alison thought she had it figured out when she saw a small spark of navy magic bloom in Emma's magic just before the ball flew at her head. Emma ducked under the ball and didn't dare try and grab onto it.

Alison was in this to win. She circled around the ball as it bounced back and forth choosing its next victim. The magic began to turn navy, and she looked around to try and see who it was targeting next. Where her eyes would normally skim over the magic, she found she was getting caught up in the details her new glasses showed her. The ball struck her in the shoulder with a sharp stinging sensation that knocked her flat on her ass. So much for winning.

A tall, broad-shouldered blonde girl pounced on the ball and wrapped her arms around it, holding onto it for dear life as the ball tried to fly up toward the ceiling. Her expression was one of grim determination. The ball's magic dissipated, leaving the girl to drop down to the floor with a broad grin blooming on her face.

"Well played," Alison said.

"Well done!"

"Congrats!"

"That was awesome!"

The other girls called. Spirits were high, and everyone wore a smile that lit up their soul energies. Alison couldn't help but match the expression as everything felt as though it were falling back into place.

CHAPTER FOUR

Leo Decker's mouth was pressed into a thin line as he looked around his library. The dark wood shelves stretched up to the arching ceiling overhead. Each row was evenly spaced and packed with books of every shape, size, and subject. He paced down the long row full of history books and slowly turned to stare at a gap on the shelf. The poppy attached to his hat bared its remarkably sharp teeth, reflecting Leo's foul mood.

The gnome was approached by another of the library's guardians, a fellow gnome dressed in the same black suit, complete with bowler hat and red poppy. The lower librarian took his bowler from his head, revealing thinning silvery hair. He played with the rim of his hat as he slowed his approach to Leo.

"We think some books were stolen, sir."

"Impossible," Leo said as he began pulling on his magic.

The very idea that someone had managed to remove books from his domain without his knowledge was absolutely ridiculous. The books were under his charge, and he made sure that they were well kept and returned on time.

He sent his magic out into the school. It would pull the book back into the library as it had done many times previously. Some students had been rather bewildered when the book had been snatched from their hands, but the due dates weren't there for idle amusement.

The spell didn't work. Leo's frown deepened, and he was joined by another gnome in the same attire. Together, the three gnomes formed the familiar spell and released their magic to search the school for the books.

Nothing.

Their magic returned to them without having so much as having touched on the books. It was as though they had vanished into the World in Between.

"Find out which books were taken," Leo barked.

Perhaps if they knew which books were gone, they'd be able to locate them. He was going to get to the bottom of this, and the magical that dared take his books would be punished.

The gnomes shut down the library and cursed out the renovations for good measure. The thief wouldn't have had an opportunity had the school have been running smoothly. A couple of small spells formed web-like threads and spread out through the school, accounting for every book bar a few history books.

"History books? They're not even specialised history. There's two on Oriceran, and one on the history of elves," Leo said, pacing back and forth.

It didn't make any sense. Someone with knowledge and skilled had taken the time to steal some history books? He was missing something, but he was determined to get those books back.

Alison was enjoying her omelette with a side of fresh fruit when the gossip seemed to explode around them.

"Books are stolen!"

"The gnomes are furious!"

"Did you hear someone stole some library books from right under the gnomes' noses?" Kathleen asked as she sat down.

"They're saying it must be a professional. No one can get a book out without the librarians knowing about it," Luke said.

Alison finished her omelette and thought this over.

"Do we know what type of books were taken?"

"Just history they think." Kathleen shrugged as her omelette appeared in front of her.

"Seriously? Why would someone take history books?" Luke asked.

"Some of us find history fascinating," a familiar British voice said.

Alison looked over to see Christie smiling at her.

"This is Christie. We met on the railroad platform. She's a freshman," Alison said, gesturing from Christie to her friends.

"I'm going to the library. I'll catch you in class," Alison said as she stood.

"I'm coming with you. I've heard so much about these gnomes. They protect those books more tightly than Fort

Knox when it had gold. And they have those weird poppies. They're magically enhanced poppies, aren't they? I mean they don't just grow that way? I thought about putting a flower in my hair, but I didn't want to look too childish," the younger girl rambled.

Alison guided her around the workers who were taking a break next to a tall ladder, drinking tea and laughing over something they saw on TV the night before. A couple of sophomores threw a glowing orb back and forth between them over the heads of the students between them. The orb gradually took on reddish-orange magic, and Alison pulled on her own magic using it to squash the orb before it became a fireball. The sophomores cursed her, but she ignored them.

"Yes, the poppies are magically enhanced, and no, I didn't think it was possible to take books without the librarians knowing. Do you know what type of history books were taken?"

"They chose gnomes because they have such strong instincts to protect their domain, didn't they? There are some really expensive books in the library, aren't there? Is it true that there's a section devoted to dark and dangerous magic?"

Alison found her inner calm and reminded herself that she was new once too. It couldn't be easy on Christie. The library was open once again and had a gnome standing guard at the doorway. Librarian Decker paced near the check-out desk with a dark expression on his face. His soul energy was full of livid reds, coppers, and oranges showing just how angry he was. Alison saw a clear seam of silver showing shame where he felt it was his fault.

"Why don't we look at the section the books were taken from? There could be a clue," Alison said, walking toward the history section.

Bounty hunting was taking down magicals who had caused harm to others but finding missing books wasn't a bad place to start practicing her skills. She was still looking for someone who had broken the laws after all.

"Is it true you can see magic and souls?"

Alison was caught off guard by that. It wasn't a conversation she wanted to have. She hadn't entirely come to terms with what she was, and Christie was still a relative stranger.

"Yeah, it is. Do you see any clues around here? I think the books should have been on this shelf somewhere. Someone said it was Oriceran history."

Christie pulled her wand out and slowly waved it back and forth in rhythmic motions while she looked at the dark wood with intense focus. Alison inspected the shelves for any strange magic. There were delicate threads and faint fingerprints where someone had worked a spell before they picked up a book, but she couldn't pick out the colors.

They slowly walked along the shelf with Alison peering at the wood and spines of the books, looking for magic and signs of exactly which books were taken. Christie kept up her spellwork with quiet whispers and a focus that formed small creases around her eyes. They bumped into an angry librarian with an equally angry poppy.

"And what do you think you're doing?" the gnome demanded.

"Nothing. I just...we..." Christie started.

"No magic in here. Don't you have class?"

"Yes, sir."

Alison said nothing. It didn't add up. Why would someone with the professional skills and knowledge put in the effort to steal some simple history books?

CHAPTER FIVE

Alison and Tanner managed to get some time alone and headed down to the kemana on a date. Alison found herself slowing her pace to enjoy the wonders of the color and magic around her. The kemana was a riot of hues. The stunning array of magic that swept out from the hub in the heart of the earth beneath the school never failed to bring a smile to her face. It was a work of art.

Tanner walked at her side with his arm casually around her waist. A quick glance showed his soul energy to be warm and contented pinks. Alison leaned into him a little, enjoying his presence. She was finally starting to feel like she had a place in this world. Her childhood had been less than ideal, pushing her to hide within the pages of books and far away worlds, but now, she had people around her to keep her grounded.

The stalls spread out around them as they reached the bottom of the glowing spiral staircase. Students and magicals wandered between the stalls and shops looking at the wares on offer. This place allowed everyone to be themselves. A tall, wispy fairy haggled with a witch over the price of a pale blue scroll. The fairy's almost ephemeral wings fluttered in increasing annoyance. Alison ran her fingertips over the back of Tanner's hand. "We should head to the scroll shop. They have a sale on."

Tanner's smile broadened. "After, we can go and eat at the elf place in the west corner. They have the best pizza for miles."

"Deal."

They strolled through the crowds, trying to ignore the furtive glances and whispers as people saw Alison and gossiped about her heritage. Tanner held her close and kept his shoulders back while Alison ignored them entirely. *Let them talk*, she thought to herself. She knew what she had done, and what she would do to keep the school safe.

The bright ribbons and webs of magic around the main thoroughfare dulled a little and formed smaller pockets of color as they made their way to the scroll shop. Alison saw the vivid gold symbols around the doorway and windows, offering far more protection than you would expect from something so simple. Through her glasses, it looked like a simple affair with a pale wooden door and a plain window displaying some plain scrolls, and some full of simple spells. Of course, she knew it was something far more interesting.

Tanner cautiously looked around and made sure no one had followed them before they stepped inside, and he released Alison. He busied himself looking through the selection of simple spell scrolls while she walked up to the counter. Beneath the easy façade, the scroll shop was a secret mail system. It was her only way of keeping in contact with Izzie. She gave the old wizard a warm smile and hoped he'd have something for her. She was missing Izzie and hoped she was doing okay.

"Good morning, do you happen to have any indigo ink and size two white scrolls?"

The wizard's lips quirked into a small smile as he understood the coded message.

"I got some in recently as it so happens," he said, rummaging through something under the thick wooden counter.

He placed a small pot of indigo ink down next to a delicate white scroll. Alison opened the scroll and was relieved to see a message from Izzie.

All is well here. We are moving around a lot, but we're comfortable. Last week, we fought a trio of dark magic elves. I'm really coming into my magic now. They underestimated me, and I kicked ass.

I ran with a pack of wolves last month. They helped harbor us in return for a favor. I wish you were here, Ali. You'd love the adventures we're having. I'm learning far more out here with my parents than I did in school.

I miss you. Hope all's well,

Izzie.

It felt as though a physical weight lifted from Alison's shoulders until she saw the message had arrived a month ago. A lot could happen in a month. She calmed down and reminded herself that it wasn't easy reaching the designated drop points, and she was clearly doing well with her parents.

The wizard placed a pen and small scroll in front of her

with a warm smile. Tanner walked to the counter and saved her from explaining that she hadn't learned to write much yet since she had gotten her new glasses.

Tanner gently kissed her temple, and they made quick work of writing a return note to Izzie telling her about their hopes for the Louper championship, and the classes they were taking that year. The wizard took the note when they were ready and disappeared into the back room. As with the other kemanas, mail was delivered via gargoyles. They carried small leather pouches via straps and could be seen if you knew where to look. It made secret notes far easier than trying to use the main mail system.

"I'm sure she'll be in touch as soon as she's able. She's probably having a blast," Tanner said reassuringly.

"Ready for that pizza?" Alison said with forced happiness.

Dwelling on things she couldn't change wasn't going to help anything. She had to live in the moment, and right then, that meant enjoying the magic of the kemana and wonderful pizza with Tanner.

The next day started without a cloud in the sky. The first class was Plants for Potions with the Light Elf, Professor Fowler. Alison and her friends sat in their usual seats and watched as the teacher carefully placed dried plants on her desk. The elf's mane of wild red hair sat halo-like around her older delicate features. It didn't matter how hard she tried to tame it; her hair remained frizzy and voluminous.

"Today, we will be making defensive potions. You will

begin with the shield forming potion from holly berries, ground oak, and sage. Those of you who master that will move onto the immobilisation potion. Is that clear?"

"Yes, Professor Fowler."

"Pair up and begin with the first potion. The recipe is on your desk. This is a simple potion that will provide a short-term shield should you find yourself under attack. It will last for roughly ten minutes, long enough to find a weapon or run—whichever your preference."

"I'd never run. I don't see why we need a shield anyway. We should just blast them," a dark-haired boy on Alison's left whispered to his friend.

She knew all too well that just blasting them wasn't always an option.

"Shields are very useful Mr. Callahan!" Ms. Fowler barked.

He looked down and blushed slightly before muttering to his friend.

"Do not underestimate the value of a well-timed shield. Now. To work."

Alison and Aya were already sitting next to each other, but Ethan leaned back and whispered, "come and work with me, Alison? We make a far better pair."

"She's not doing your work for you, Ethan," Aya said.

"You should be working, Ethan," the teacher scolded as she walked between the rows of desks.

"Kathleen, the recipe clearly states you are to warm the berries not roast them with your magic gently."

"It was more efficient my way," the red-headed girl said.

"It was a waste of berries. Now you have dissolved the important magic within them and overrode it with your own. That will form nothing more than a transparent film that anyone could step through without thought or effort. Your haste could have gotten you or a friend killed."

"That's a little harsh don't you think?" Peter asked.

"Life is a little harsh. Please don't try and add your science into this. I see the iron filing in your hand."

"She's taking this really seriously," Aya whispered as Alison watched the gently curling wisps of pale green magic wrapping around the berries.

"Everyone's on edge since the attack last semester," she said just before she pulled the berries from the small flame and carefully dropped them into the beaker.

The distinct smell of burning wood and ash permeated the room, and Alison wrinkled her nose.

"You are to scatter the oak on the berries in the beaker!"

"They are in the beaker."

Alison leaned over a little and saw that Ben had misread the recipe. He was holding the beaker over the small, red flames with the berries and oak inside it. The oak was smoldering, and together, it produced thin shards of navy blue magic.

"Take the beaker off the fire before it forms something you will have to clean up."

"So much for a simple recipe," Aya muttered.

They gently crushed the berries and warm oak together with a slender wooden spoon before they added the dried sage. The smell was slightly sweet with an acidic edge that almost hurt Alison's nose. She watched in wonder as the magic within turned an odd white with a lilac sheen.

"Is it right, Alison?"

"Yes, it looks perfect," she said with a grin.

Kathleen glared at her berries and oak mix as she took her annoyance out on them, and Ben was scrubbing furiously at the black tar on his desk. If this were a situation where they really needed the shields, they'd have been in deep trouble.

"Well, don't just sit there; try out the shield. Take a pinch of the powder and rub it between your thumb and forefinger while visualising a bubble," Professor Fowler said.

Alison and Aya shared a look before Alison reached into the beaker and pulled out a pinch of the powder. It felt oddly pliable. She had expected a silky dust sensation, but it was almost leathery. Taking a slow breath, she rubbed the dust between her finger and thumb and pictured a clear bubble forming around her. Her Drow magic started swelling within her eager to join in the spell. She lost the image of the bubble and frowned.

"Try again. Control is everything."

Once again, she picked up a pinch of the dust and formed the image of a bubble in her mind. Slowly the off-white magic spread outward in a shimmery circle which suddenly popped up into a bubble. It expanded around her hand, her arm, then her chest. Something wasn't quite right. She couldn't make it go around her entire body. Alison poked the shimmering white shield and was glad to see that it was solid.

"Hold onto the image, Alison," Professor Fowler said.

She looked at the magic and slowly exhaled while pushing the image in her mind down over the lower half. It didn't budge, but it remained where it was.

"Use a little less oak next time. You've made it too rigid. Who's next?" Professor Fowler said.

Alison reached out with her Drow magic and popped the bubble with an audible sound. Ethan turned around. "I knew you could do it. You're the most talented person in here."

"I wouldn't say that," Alison said.

CHAPTER SIX

The sun had set a few hours prior, and Alison found herself unable to sleep. She rolled over and looked out the window at the magic from the stars in the clear night sky. The other girls were all fast asleep. She stood and glanced over at Izzie's empty bed, a pang of heartache hit her. They used to take midnight strolls together to talk about whatever was on their mind. Tonight, she'd have to do it alone.

Alison dressed quickly and left her glasses behind. She wanted the familiarity of seeing the magic without the distractions of seeing everything else too. The path through the sleeping house was one she had walked silently many times before, meaning she was soon outside under the open night sky. The stars were singing that night. The thin slivers of silver magic wove around them forming a delicate tapestry that made her smile. She stood looking up at the large expanse of sky for a little while before she needed to move again.

Izzie was out in the world somewhere, likely being

pursued by dark and dangerous people. Alison knew that she was with her family, and she was happy for her, but that didn't erase the worry that squirmed in her gut. It had been a month since her last note from Izzie. What if the worst had happened? The thought swirled around Alison's mind as she meandered across the gently undulating lawn around the grounds. Her feet carried her toward the stables with the familiar warm scents of hay, straw, and horses.

Something caught her eye, a flash of crimson against the darkness. It was quickly coupled with a second ribbon of garnet, and she recognized the lust for what it was. A pair of students were enjoying the privacy of the haybarn where they could sate their lust without any interference. Alison hurried away not wanting to get involved in that particular conversation. She made her way into the woods with the tall, strong lines of deep green and brown forming the trees around her. Small fluttering orbs of baby blues were nestled up high beneath the canopy where small birds and such were sleeping.

Nothing was the same since the big fight. The tension and worry that it would happen again draped over the entire school like a thick blanket that was almost suffocating. There was a small glimmer of slate grey present within all the teachers, a concern that gnawed at them. Mostly they put on a brave face and smile for the students, but Alison could see it.

Maybe she'd go and talk to Horace. The old groundskeeper always provided an ear when the students needed to talk. It would have been nice to talk about her thoughts and get her feelings out rather than keeping them bottled up.

Something drew her out of her thoughts. There was a book lying between a pair of broad trees off the beaten path. Alison approached it and looked around for any signs of who might have dropped it. There were no other people around, but there was a faint trail of magic. She crouched and inspected the magic clinging to the cream pages to make sure it wasn't a bizarre trap. The magic was dark orange with smudges of yellows. It looked like dirty finger-prints running across the pages. She picked it up and felt a slight warmth as though it had been sitting in the sun.

The trail of magic became clear as she held the book. It appeared to be a glittering orange sequence of small orbs that ran between the trees and out into the fields. Alison smiled, happy to finally have a lead on the case of the missing books. It wasn't quite a bad wizard, but it was a start. She followed the trail between the trees and out through the thick, lush grass of the fields up over the gentle rise of the hill.

It curved around to the east and led her down by the streams and around the edge of the teacher's cottages which were strictly out of bounds. The trail flickered, and Alison picked up the pace almost jogging as she passed around the back of the main mansion. A couple of lights shone from behind curtains on the upper floors. Two silhouettes gestured angrily at each other before one left. Alison wasn't the only one unable to sleep.

She ran through the grass and found herself back at the main driveway. The trail flickered and started to dim as she ran after it. She came to a sharp stop when the orbs vanished right where she'd picked the book up an hour or so ago. Alison looked around trying to see what she had missed. She'd just gone in an entire circle and found nothing. Someone was toying with her, and she was going to find out who.

Alison held the book in front of her and slowed her breathing, allowing her Drow magic to come forward. There had to be more to the magic, something she hadn't seen. She was going to get to the bottom of this. Her Drow magic flowed easily into her fingertips and through her chest. She maintained control only allowing a small piece to run over the spine of the book. Something sparked. Brilliant bright orange was vivid against the darkness of the forest around her. It was there then gone.

The rest of the lingering magic slipped away. Alison tried to hold it tight with her magic, but it ran between her fingers like thin trickles of water. No matter what she did, she couldn't hold it there.

"Fine. If the magic won't tell me anything then maybe the book will," she said to herself as she leaned against the closest tree.

Pressing her fingertips to the first page, she activated the braille spell and ran her fingers down the index. It was a general history book from early Earth. There wasn't anything even slightly related to magic within its covers. Refusing to give in just yet, she flipped through the pages feeling for something unusual. Maybe it wasn't a normal book. Maybe it had been used to hide something other than words.

A page was missing. Just one. It took her a few minutes to figure out that it sat between a chapter on the American's role in World War One and the aftermath of said role. She ran her tongue over her teeth feeling frustration rise. Nothing about this made any sense.

She wished Izzie was there to talk this through with her. Izzie always had a fun and different perspective that often revealed things Alison would never find on her own. She sighed and walked out of the woods looking over to the groundskeeper's cottage. Maybe Horace would have some insight.

The dragon, Dorvu, was sprawled out on the grass in front of Horace and his aunt, Estelle. Alison smiled as she watched the dragon's soul take on a rose-pink blush as Horace rubbed the dragon's forehead.

"He's not a cat, Horace."

"I'm aware of that, but he thrives on attention."

Dorvu stretched and shook out his wings shooting Estelle a slit-eyed look before he walked a few steps away.

"Bored," he declared.

"What about those rabbits you've been hunting?"

"They're learning. I can't chase them in circles any more, and the squirrels just chitter at me," Dorvu huffed.

The dragon looked at the stables and took a step closer.

"Don't you dare go hassling those horses," Horace scolded.

Dorvu blew out a frosty breath, forming a small patch of white frozen grass. The dragon tilted his head slightly as he looked at the grass.

"I don't like that look…"

The dragon didn't say anything before he flapped his great wings and took off toward the main mansion.

"He's trouble," Estelle said between drags on her cigarette.

Horace and his aunt fell into a conversation as Alison approached, and she changed paths back toward bed. It was better not to interrupt, and she could solve this problem by herself. She was sure of it.

"Alison, hi!" a familiar British voice called down the hallway.

Alison stopped by the doorway to the Plants for Potions lab and waited for Christie to make her way through the crowds. The younger witch had a broad grin plastered on her face and her hair tied in a low ponytail. She clutched her book bag to her hip as she tried to squeeze between a group of older boys who all towered a foot over her and didn't notice her. She bumped straight into one and flushed bright red.

"Look where you're going," the boy said gruffly.

"Try looking down every now and again," Christie retorted.

The boys laughed and started to form a circle around her, but a glare from Professor Fowler put a stop to that.

"Alison, hi! How have you been? Did you see that the dragon frosted the teacher's windows and doors closed last night? Is he normally like that? How did he even get here? I thought dragons were really terrifying creatures like in the myths, but that one seems really cool," Christie said in a rush of words.

"Hi, how're you settling in?" Alison asked, having missed half of what Christie had said.

"Oh, you know. New schools are always weird, especially one like this. The rooms are better than I expected, and the classes are pretty fun so far. There's not as much homework as I thought there would be, but I guess there's lots of time for assigned reading, right?"

They made their way out toward the back of the mansion where they could have a little peace and quiet before classes began in earnest.

"Yeah, the rooms are pretty nice here. Don't worry. The teachers will heap homework on you soon. Are you really looking forward to homework?"

"Well, no, but I do love reading and learning, and homework gives me a chance to do that. You know?"

"I hadn't thought about it like that."

They sat on a small wooden bench overlooking the forested foothills of the mountains.

"Have you heard anything more about those missing books? They're history books, right? Do you know what type of history yet? Someone said it was just human history, but that doesn't make any sense at all? And how did they get past the gnomes? No one can figure that out."

Alison frowned at her unsure if the younger witch should be involved in things like this.

"I snuck into the library after hours last night to have another look. I know we looked, and you didn't see any weird magic, but I needed to see if there was something hidden."

"You would have been in deep trouble if you'd have been caught."

"I didn't find anything, have you?"

Alison looked at the effervescent girl and decided that telling her a little wouldn't do any harm. She wasn't sure that bringing her into the full investigation was a good idea.

"I found one of the books last night, but it didn't lead anywhere. There were no clues. It was weird."

"So, they're a real pro then?"

"I guess. Why would a pro be interested in some mundane history books though? It makes no sense."

"Maybe they weren't interested in those books? What if that was just a test run?"

Alison looked at Christie. She might be onto something there. She'd been assuming that those books were the target, but what if it was the start of something much bigger?

CHAPTER SEVEN

The school was buzzing with excitement for the first Louper game of the year. The Cardinals were up against the Wichita Lions. It was Luke's first match as team captain, and he wasn't going to let the school down. He glanced up at the stands seeing Aya, Emma, Tanner, and the others all sitting together ready to cheer them on. Izzie should have been up there with them. The shifter looked away and tried to quell the feeling of loneliness and sadness that washed over him. Izzie was strong, and she'd be ok out there.

"Get your heads in the game team! Remember single-ness of purpose! We're strong, fast, and we're in this to win!"

Dan, a sophomore, stood at Luke's side, a little bedrag-gled, but hardness and determination were in his eyes. They weren't just playing to win for themselves. They were fighting to give the school hope. Luke looked around his team. A couple new faces smiled back at him. A slender, brunette, female wood elf named Shannon, with piercing slate-grey eyes, stared straight at him, challenging him. The first female on the team in years. Luke bared his teeth a little, feeling his wolf rise. The elf smirked and looked away.

"Remember, we work as a team!" Luke growled.

The elf lowered her eyes and composed herself. She hadn't intended to upset the team captain. She was merely showing she wasn't afraid of him as a shifter. She wasn't some weak girl. She was here to kick ass and get them through to the finals along with the guys.

"The Lions won't screw around. You need to bring your A-game. Are you with me?"

Luke looked at each of his team members in turn, and a swell of pride filled him. They were fit and skilled. They were going all the way this year.

The spell was cast, and the field vanished around them, leaving them in a frozen wasteland. They were in the Yukon territory, a stretch of white with slices of grey cutting up toward an icy blue sky. It was barren and flat with nothing but great blades of grey rock breaking up the sea of white. Shannon slowly turned in a circle looking for some clue as to what they were supposed to do. The snowy landscape was far away from her natural habitat, but that wasn't going to slow her down.

Ethan stepped away from Luke and put his hand above his eyes, shielding them from the harsh sunlight before he grinned triumphantly.

"There! There's a glint of gold there!"

The team turned to look at where Ethan pointed. Sure enough, there was something glinting bright gold at the very tip of the rocky outcrop. To their dismay, the yellow jerseys of the Lions were racing across the ice and snow toward the very same outcrop.

"Get moving!" Luke yelled.

They took off across the flat expanse as quickly as they could manage without losing their footing on the thin layer of snow over the ice below. They never took their eyes off the gold as they gave it everything they had.

White clouds puffed out in front of each of them as they slowed, the cold air filling their lungs and stealing away the oxygen. The yellow jerseys of the Lions were out of sight, but they couldn't have reached the outcrop yet. A rumbling sound cut through the eerie quiet around them, and Luke's ears pricked. His shifter instincts told him something bad was coming.

"Bear!" Dan shouted.

The full-blooded wizard pulled his wand and turned to face the enraged grizzly barrelling toward them.

"We can take it."

"We definitely can't out run it!"

They stopped and turned to face the great bear. The closer it got, the more apparent its long claws and huge paws became. Its long white teeth were made for tearing. They were all too aware of how much power hid within those thick massive muscles, and its dense, brown hide meant it was practically a tank.

"We can't use physical force. We need to use our magic to destroy it," Ethan said.

Luke was familiar with how erratic Ethan's magic could be.

"Shannon, combine your magic with Ethan's. Control

and direct it. Blast that bear in the chest, and knock it on its ass," Luke said.

The elf gave a small nod to Ethan. Together, they called on their magic and directed it toward the bear. Ethan's mouth pinched in concentration as he tried to put everything he'd learned into practice. He knew he could do this. Calm and focus.

Shannon's magic flew straight and true at the bear's heart with Ethan's own pure white magic right behind it. The elf pushed away all distractions and focused on the feeling of her magic guiding Ethan's. He had a lot of power, but she struggled to corral it. The bear was almost within mauling distance. They only had one chance at this.

The crowd in the stands was silent as they watched the bear. Alison gripped Tanner's hand tight as she couldn't look away. Everyone erupted into cheers when the bear evaporated, leaving nothing but a puff of white breath where it had been.

"Well done team. Now, let's get moving," Luke said.

They'd lost precious time, and who knew how far ahead the Lions were now. Wanting to preserve precious energy, they set off at a steady lope rather than a flat-out sprint. The rockface looked like a difficult climb, and they were going to need every bit of strength they could muster.

After what felt like hours of running, they reached a wide river with white rapids thrashing around a set of stepping stones. Each stone was a small island amidst the white foam and fury of the icy water. The stones were entirely flat and smooth and evenly spaced in a neat line across the river. It was a trap. They just didn't know quite what type of trap.

"There's magic wrapped around the stones," Dan said cautiously.

"Do you see another way around?" Ethan asked.

"We can swim," Rex, another new player suggested.

Everyone ignored him. There was no way they'd be able to swim across those rapids. They'd be crushed against the rocks and drowned before they knew what had happened.

"I'll go first," Shannon volunteered.

"No, I will. I'm the captain and a shifter. I move faster than you," Luke said.

It was his job to lead his team, and that meant taking risks like this. He had to show them the way.

His instincts told him speed was key. His heart pounded in his chest as he leapt off the bank onto the first stone step. Nothing happened. He leapt onto the next and quickly got into a rhythm finding himself on the far side without any trouble.

"Come on. Quickly!" he called.

Ethan was next. His crossing wasn't quite as smooth as Luke's had been, but it went without a hitch. It was when he leapt onto the final stone that everyone saw what the trap was. The stones sank a few inches. They were still passable, but it was more difficult.

"Go! Now!" Dan said, pushing Shannon.

She leapt onto the first stone and felt it dip beneath her. She wasted no time in jumping from stone to stone, pushing aside her fear as the cold water splashed against her legs and reminded her just how close the end was. Dan and Rex were hot on her heels.

Rex's foot slipped on the second to last stone, and his eyes went wide as he looked at the frothing white around him. His heart jumped into his throat, and he lost his confidence. Luke jumped across the stones and grabbed onto him, pulling him to safety just as the stones vanished beneath the water. They lay panting on the dark-grey gravel.

"Thanks, man," Rex said.

"It's what the team's all about," Luke said.

The cold was sinking into their bones slowing them down, but the Lions were advancing. They saw them swarming around the base of the grey rock.

"They're going straight up!" Shannon said in awe.

The climb up the face of the outcrop was brutal. It was almost fully vertical with mostly smooth stone to try and find grips on.

"Don't worry about them. We're taking the east route up the side," Luke said, nodding to the path formed between shards of stone. It wasn't easy, but they had a far better chance than scaling the sheer rock.

Ethan stepped out in front of Luke. "I can do this. I climbed a lot when I was younger."

The shifter smiled and stepped back, giving him a clear route to the top. His friend deserved the glory of getting the disk, and he wasn't going to let his pride get in the way of the goal—winning the match.

They jumped up from the thick gravel below and grasped onto the thin ledge of rock just above them. Shannon helped Rex up onto the ledge, her upper body strength proving better than his.

"You just lost to a girl." She smirked.

Rex rolled his eyes. "I was just letting you look good."

"Whatever you say."

They made their way up the grueling path, half climbing and half walking up through the layers of grey rock. The cold was making their fingers numb as they sought out good grips and helped each other climb. The gold disk was almost within sight, but so were the Lions.

The leader of the Lions, a lanky shifter with unruly blonde hair, hung by his fingertips with his body dangling free from a steep angled part of the climb. His face was growing paler as he struggled to find footing and failed. Eventually, he lost his grip entirely and fell, disappearing from the game.

A gasp went out through the crowd. The Cardinals were within a hair of the disk now, but the Lions were right there with them. No one dared look away as they watched Luke and his team slowly make their way up the most difficult part of the climb. The path had narrowed to almost nothing. Their limbs were growing heavy, and the light was fading.

Thick swathes of color lazily cut across the increasingly dark blue sky as the aurora began for the night. It was a beautiful display with soft pinks and rich greens sweeping across the expanse of sky in a casual dance that had been happening for millennia. The Cardinals didn't pay any attention to that. Their minds were occupied with the need to find the next grip, the next foot hold.

They were so close that Ethan could almost reach out and grab the gold disk where it rested on the very precipice of the rock. The sharp stone was weathered into a vicious point. Ethan's foot slipped out from under him, and he yelped in surprise as all his weight was suddenly shifted onto his arms.

"I have you," Luke said as he grabbed Ethan's shirt and pushed him up.

"Thanks, dude," Ethan panted.

"Come on. Don't give up on us now!" Shannon called.

The Cardinals were breathing hard. A small stone skittered down the cliff face, reminding everyone just how far they'd come. Ethan gritted his teeth and dug deep for one last burst of energy. He stretched out for a difficult hand hold. His fingers almost slipped from the numbness, but he pressed harder and got it. With one almighty push, he stretched out his other hand and grabbed the gold disk.

They'd done it. They'd won.

The snowy landscape vanished around them, and they collapsed onto the familiar field to the roars of celebration and pride from the stands. They gulped down warm air and reveled in the feeling of having won the first match of the year.

CHAPTER EIGHT

The buzz from the win over the Wichita Lions was still filling the air as everyone filed into the History of Magic class. Professor Hudson watched as they laughed and jostled each other finding their preferred seats. She was pleased to see them in such high spirits after the game. There was a tangible weight hanging over the school which the renovations only added to. They were a constant reminder of what had happened the previous semester.

"Settle down. Now, who can tell me about the Easter island, Moai?"

She looked at the students' confused expressions. After an almost painful silence, Alison slowly lifted her hand.

"That's the local name for the large heads that have confused humans for centuries," she said quietly.

"Yes! Who knows the real history behind them?"

The students looked around at each other. Some shrugged, and others studiously looked down at their desks and refused to look at Professor Hudson.

"Does anyone know the human ideas around them at

least?"

"They think the heads are something religious, and the indigenous peoples wiped themselves out through mismanagement of their surroundings," Aya said.

"Yes, thank you, Aya."

The professor leaned back against her desk, crossing her arms as she prepared to tell them the bloody history of the island.

"Many centuries ago, the island was a wild place." She looked around making sure everyone was listening. "There was a small human population present. They were more aware of the magicals within their environment than most other humans of the time. This led to them forming a simple religion around a small rift that was hidden at the very heart of the island. Just beneath the volcano, a small pocket of very potent magic had formed and leaked out into the island. The humans weren't aware on a conscious level of what was happening, but they knew they needed to protect it."

Luke yawned and stretched his legs out beneath his desk while Kathleen chewed on her pen cap, waiting for this to get interesting.

"A small group of elves made their way onto the island. Understanding the potential present, they worked with the humans to enlighten them and show them the possibilities within their world. The humans were awe-struck and easily manipulated by the elves. Unfortunately, humans from surrounding areas including Polynesia were becoming interested in the island. The well of magic buried beneath the volcano called to them."

Alison listened with rapt attention. It reminded her of

one of her adventures that she'd read as a little girl.

"The elves knew they needed to be able to defend the island from intruders. The primitive weapons of the humans weren't going to be enough. And so, they forged the statues you see today. They were guardians capable of moving with great speed when needed. The statues proved to be formidable protectors and kept the island safe for a century. Unfortunately, over that time dissent formed between the humans and the elves.

"The elves were growing greedy. They viewed humans as beneath them, and as the generations of humans passed, each one was more aware of the magic. It was bleeding into their beings. They were incapable of using it, but it gave them a determination and desire to protect. Soon, that desire turned to war.

"If you read the human ideas on the history of this place, you will stumble across references to the long ears and short ears. It is assumed that the long ears are invading Polynesians. They were the elves, and sadly the humans wiped them out taking the magic from the stone guardians with them. The balance of the island was destroyed, and soon the humans were destroyed with it."

"That's so badass!" Ethan exclaimed.

"It's sort of interesting I suppose," Kathleen said.

"We should learn from history. What can we take away from this?" Professor Hudson pushed.

"Don't screw with elves?" Luke asked.

Everyone laughed.

The professor shook her head.

"Everything is fleeting, and we should enjoy what time we have," Emma said.

"Way to keep it cheerful," a broad-shouldered wizard muttered.

Professor Hudson felt the focus of her class slipping away from her.

"Tell me, what is it you'll do with this time you have?"

She hoped that perhaps if she could direct them to think about their futures, then she'd be able to steer them back to the past. It was all interlinked after all.

"Alison, what are your career plans?"

The Drow felt her spine straighten in pride as she said, "I'm going to follow in my father's footsteps and become a bounty hunter. I haven't decided if I'll go to college first."

She spoke with far more confidence than she had done when she first came to the school. There was an edge to her that came with her control over her magic. Professor Hudson could see her making a fine bounty hunter.

"I'm going into fashion," a pretty blonde witch called.

"I'm going to create a business empire forging magic and science," Peter chimed in.

"Assuming you don't blow yourself up first." Ethan nudged his friend.

"All part of the process." Peter grinned.

"I'm going to work for the government." A bold teenager with white streaks through his dark hair raised his hand.

Silence fell over the classroom.

"You want to work with the human government? You're going to turn against your own people!?" a shifter growled.

"The humans just want to control us and take whatever they can get their hands on. They know nothing but war and destruction. Why would you help them?"

"We can work with them to improve the balance. We can make the worlds better places," the boy explained.

"You're stupider than you look if you think you can change the government." Luke scowled at him.

"Maybe he's onto something. How can we expect to bring about change if we don't get involved?" a red-haired girl said timidly.

"You're throwing your own people under the bus if you join the government. They can't be trusted. They'll tear us apart and experiment on us if they see an opportunity."

Alison frowned and looked around at the growing anger throughout the room. Students' soul energies flickered with reds and burgundies where their passion and anger at the idea filled them.

"You're ridiculous! You've watched too many movies. The government just wants to do what's best for the worlds."

"And you're naive to believe such a thing. The government exists solely to continue its own existence and grow its own power," the elf snapped as she stood up and slammed her hands on the desk.

Professor Hudson stood and held up her hand. The students paused then settled themselves back into their seats.

"That is quite enough. You have thoroughly demonstrated how quickly it can become them versus us."

A flush of shame passed over Aya as she realized she had been ready to join in the argument. She knew better than to view the world as black and white, but sometimes it was so easy to do.

CHAPTER NINE

Alison slipped away from her friends after lunch and wove her way through the corridors to the library where she met Tanner. He grinned at her, the thrill of doing something they shouldn't exactly be doing added electricity to his veins.

Leo Decker frowned at the approaching couple, and his poppy blew a raspberry at them.

"Good afternoon, Librarian Decker. We were hoping you'd be able to answer a few questions for us," Alison said.

The gnome narrowed his eyes a little. They were up to no good. He just knew it.

"And what questions would those be?"

"Well, we heard that a few books were taken from here…"

The gnome straightened his jacket and sniffed.

"And?"

"Well, would you be able to tell us which books were taken?"

"And why would I do that?"

Alison wasn't sure where to go from there. She couldn't really tell him that she planned on finding the thief herself.

"We believe that we may be able to help with your investigation. Alison's father is Mr. Brownstone, the bounty hunter. She is quite experienced with tracking down-"

"Save your breath. I know what you're trying to say. We are, however, making progress with our investigations," Leo said as he glanced back at the shelves with the missing books.

They were entirely clueless, and that galled him. Who would put in such effort to steal a couple of simple history books?

"Oh? So, you know who the thief is?" Tanner asked.

The tension in the gnome's jaw, and the fact no one had been named told him that the gnomes had no idea who'd taken the books. He had, however, spoken to the head-mistress and Professor Powell and found out that two more books had been taken. If they could get Leo to talk, then he was sure they'd have a pattern.

"No. Not yet."

"Then why don't you let us help?" Alison asked.

"They took books on human world history, and one on the history of shifter magic and transfiguration," one of the other gnomes said from behind the front desk.

Leo glared at the traitorous gnome, making him shrink back behind the desk.

"Thank you so much for your help," Alison said.

They hurried out of the library.

"The thief was looking into transfiguration. All of the books had ties to transfiguration and changing the magical state of a person." Alison was excited to have a lead.

"Who would want to do that? It sounds incredibly dangerous."

"Someone who's unhappy with their magic."

Alison ran the thoughts through her mind. It was clearly someone who wanted to change. Could it have been a human who wanted to become a magical? That wasn't unheard of. Humans were sometimes caught with dangerous artifacts when they wanted to wield magic. That didn't explain how they got around the gnomes though, and humans were few and far between on the grounds. It was a school for the magical. Everyone would have seen a human sneaking books out of the library. No, it had to be a magical of some form.

"What about a shifter?" Tanner offered.

"Perhaps, but they have no innate magic of their own. They couldn't do it alone."

"We're looking for more than one person?"

"Maybe. We need more information, but this is a good start!"

"You look beautiful when you're fired up like this." Tanner took Alison's hands into his.

His soul glowed with happiness that was reflected in Alison's own soul.

"You're going to be an excellent bounty hunter, and your dad will be incredibly proud."

Alison rushed to the auditorium, hoping she wasn't too late

for the auditions for Wicked. Professor Fowler had already announced that she was going to let people know what parts they won during the audition.

Alison was looking forward to taking part in the musicals although a pang of sadness hit her as she stepped into the room. Usually, Izzie would be there with her, no matter what they were doing. Her best friend had a beautiful voice and a huge presence, meaning she took the lead part. Alison pushed aside the sadness. She was going to give it her all.

Kathleen and Emma waved to Alison and ushered her over to the corner of the stage where they watched a sophomore wizard sing off key. They took a seat in the front row as the boy put his heart and soul into the awful rendition. He started gesturing with his hands, adding more presence to his vocals, and it made it worse.

"I think it'd be best if he stuck to debate club," Kathleen whispered.

The boy missed the top note, and it came out as an awful noise that made Alison cringe.

"Maybe he can do the scenery," Emma said diplomatically.

As he walked toward them with his head hung low, it was easy to see that he wouldn't be getting a part, Alison recognized him. He was in the Young Entrepreneurs club with Peter. If she remembered right, he'd been the one to give Peter the idea of trying to infuse magic with robots to make small automatons. Kathleen had given him a big lecture about how that would bring about the end of the world, had he never seen The Terminator?

"Which part are you going for?" Emma asked.

"Elphaba," Alison said, quashing the butterflies forming in her stomach.

"I've seen some good Elphabas. Sarah, you know the half witch with the green streak in her hair? She really wowed the teachers," Kathleen said as they looked at Professor Fowler who was frowning at a list on her clipboard.

"No one has been declared Elphaba yet," Emma said as she squeezed Alison's hand in comfort.

"I'm trying for Glinda," Kathleen said.

"You really think you can pull off a good witch?" Alison teased.

Kathleen ignored her before her scowl cracked, and she laughed.

"Of course, I will," Kathleen said before she strode out onto the stage.

True to form Kathleen sang with confidence and power that made it an easy decision for the teachers. She was born to play the role of Glinda.

Everyone watching the auditions clapped and cheered, which only encouraged Kathleen to bow and play up to them. She blew a kiss before she strutted back to her friends.

"Christie Bealls," Professor Fowler called.

Christie steeled herself and made her way over to the center of the stage. She'd dreamt of being in the musical, but now she wasn't sure if she had the talent. What if she made a fool out of herself?

Alison frowned as she saw an odd spark within Christie's magic that she swore hadn't been there before. It was a heather grey spark sitting just above the crown of her head. After a moment, she shrugged it off, thinking it must have been residue from the girl's previous class.

"Which part are you auditioning for, Christie?"

"Madamee Morrible"

A hush fell over the auditorium. No one expected a freshman to be able to get such a pivotal role. Two seniors had already auditioned for the part and put in strong performances. Whispers passed through the students saying that Anne was a sure thing for Madame Morrible.

"When you're ready," the professor said.

Christie took a slow, steadying breath and closed her eyes as the music began. Singing was something she had been doing since she was a little girl. It had become an escape of sorts, losing herself in the music.

She began a little shaky and quiet, but after a few bars, her confidence grew and her voice with it. Everyone watched on in awe as Christie sang with a depth of emotion and power that no one had seen coming. She was talented, far more than anyone would have guessed. When she finished the song, she opened her eyes to see a standing ovation. Alison joined in and called out her congratulations.

"And we have found our Madame Morrible." Professor Fowler grinned.

The cheers and clapping grew even louder before the professor waved at them to be quiet. Christie was overwhelmed. She'd never sung on a stage in front of people like that before. Adrenaline filled her and made it feel as though she were walking on clouds when she walked across the stage. She'd done it.

"Alison Brownstone."

Alison took her place in the center of the stage and steadied her hands as she ran the lyrics through her head. She could do this.

"When you're ready."

She took a deep breath and began singing with all her heart. She visualised Izzie in the audience watching and giving her support. Her best friend wasn't there in person, but she was sure she was there in spirit. The performance was flawless as Alison gave herself over to the music.

"And we have our Elphaba! The remaining auditionees will sing on the chorus or be given a place on the scenery team. Congratulations, everyone. I'm sure this will be the best musical yet!" The professor said, standing and grinning on.

Mutters and comments passed around the crowd, and Alison received some dark glares. It was clear that some people felt she wasn't right for the leading role. Alison ignored them. She'd worked hard to refine her voice, and she was ready to take center stage. She'd do it for Izzie.

The professor's tightly braided hair stood in stark contrast to the violent, purple plaid pants she had chosen to wear. She made her way between the chairs and called the chosen students up onto the stage. The musical was going to be a lot of hard work, but she knew some of the students from previous productions. She was sure it would be a spectacular show.

"Come along. Practice begins tomorrow. Start learning your lines tonight. Christie and Alison, you have a lot of lines together. Make sure to work together and help each other out." She thrust the sheets with Alison's lines into her hands.

Emma and Kathleen gathered around Alison and put their arms around her shoulders.

"I'm proud of you," Emma said.

She'd watched her friend go from a quiet girl to the confident woman next to her. Still, she hadn't missed the darkness that hung over Alison. There seemed to be a small shadow in her eyes that had formed during the big fight at the end of the last semester. The musical would give them something positive to focus on, an escape from the tension and invisible weight hanging over the school.

"We'll be practicing together. Won't that be fun!" Christie said as she beamed at Alison.

"We met at breakfast, right? You're a freshman at the school?" Kathleen asked.

"This is Christie." Alison gestured toward Kathleen. The redhead looked at the freshman. "This is Kathleen, one of my best friends."

"Well, it's nice to meet you, again. If you'll excuse me, I want to talk to the professor."

Christie noticeably deflated, and Alison guided her away to a quiet corner where they could speak freely.

"Sorry, Kathleen's a great friend, but she can be... like that."

"It's okay. Everyone treats me like that, really. I haven't really made any friends. People ignore me or push me away because I'm different. I know that I'm not from a prestigious family, and I have a weird accent. It'll be ok."

Alison put her hand on the girl's shoulder, offering her comfort. She hated seeing her looking quite so down. She had grown used to her enthusiasm and effervescence.

"Well, then that's their loss. You sang beautifully earlier, too."

Christie visibly brightened.

"Thanks! I've been singing since I was a little girl. There's something really relaxing about it. I feel like I'm finally at peace when I sing. The music washes over me, and everything else slips away. It's like I step into a better world. One where everything's beautiful, and I can be myself without worrying about anything."

Alison smiled at the rush of words.

"Why don't we try and practice after dinner? Do you think you'll have time?"

"Yes, the homework isn't too bad. I'd love to, and you're going to make an amazing Elphaba. There's so much passion in your singing that I know you'll knock everyone's socks off."

The girl's soul glowed a warm, pale orange where she was relaxing once more. Alison was looking forward to spending more time with her. She was so enthusiastic that it was addictive in an odd way.

"What made you choose the role of Madame Morrible?"

"Oh, that's easy! Madame Morrible is such a huge character she's amazing fun to play, and she has the best costumes. Everything about her is so extreme and over the top that I can really slip into being someone else with her. I don't agree with how manipulative and horrible she is of course, but I think she's a fascinating character. What about you? Why did you choose Elphaba?"

Alison thought about it for a moment.

"I guess because there's a likeness there, between her

and me. I mean… I'm different, and that means I get weird looks, and I'm not always understood."

The more she thought on it; the more she saw the reflection of her own frustrations and feelings at not being able to do enough in the world. There was a sensation that there were forces outside of her control pushing and tugging at her. She was fighting to find her own path, but her heritage meant that people judged her based purely on that and her looks.

"Because you're a Drow right? I think that's really cool. You can see soul energies and magic, too, right? Wait. I already asked that, didn't I?"

Alison laughed "Yes. That was all I could see before my mom got these glasses for me. I'm still adjusting to seeing the world."

"Wow, what does that look like?"

"A beautiful kaleidoscope of color. Everything has its own specific color. I often feel as though it's everyone else that's blind."

CHAPTER TEN

Alison, Ethan, Emma, and Luke ran in a crouch, trying to hide from prying eyes as they slipped behind the bushes and started sprinting away from the school. Their hearts were pounding in their chests as they reached the Chevette—their getaway vehicle. They piled in with Emma squeezing next to Alison in the cramped back seat. Laughter and excitement filled the car as they shot off the school grounds and headed toward Charlottesville.

It felt good to break the rules sometimes, and it wasn't as if they were doing something dangerous. They just needed a little time away to be among the bright lights and vibrancy of the town. Alison relaxed as she looked out of the partially open window and breathed in the fresh cool air. The rolling green fields slowly gave way to beautiful buildings with large, cream pillars and red brick. They looked regal sitting behind their neatly trimmed lawns and immaculately designed flower beds. She was glad to have her glasses on, so she could see the technicolor splendor of the town.

People crowded the sidewalks as they left the human schools and jobs. They were all bundled up in their sweaters and boots. Fall was clearly in the air. The trees took on copper and gold hues as the tips of their foliage began to turn for winter. That didn't stop the late flowering plants that overflowed the large, wooden barrels interspersed between the mature trees. Bold splashes of red, purple, and pink tumbled over the well-worn greying wood of the barrels. There was nothing dull about the town.

Ethan parked the car in a small parking lot near the mall. and they all tumbled out with grins on their faces. It felt good to have a little freedom.

Luke stretched, and his grin only widened when he saw a burger restaurant at the end of the block.

"It's been too long since I sank my teeth into a good burger." He patted his stomach as it growled.

"You ate an hour ago!" Emma laughed.

"I'm a growing boy." Luke grinned.

"You're certainly something," Ethan returned.

Luke nudged his friend with his elbow. "You can come and join me in the gym. You have to have some muscles in there somewhere."

"I have muscles," Ethan said, flexing his bicep.

Luke peered at his arm with narrowed eyes.

"If I look really closely, I think I see something..."

Emma rolled her eyes.

"We should get a milkshake. There's a new place that opened over the summer. They're supposed to have every flavor you could ever want."

"Everyone knows the only good milkshake is chocolate," Ethan said.

They headed down the sidewalk as a tight-knit group, making their way between the locals. Alison looked at them all with a broad smile. There was just so much to see. If she'd have been without her glasses, their souls would have been a plain yellow. Now, she saw the bright crimson of one woman's coat and how it clashed with her electric blue spiked hair. Emma steered her around a slow-moving older man who was too focused on his phone call to notice Alison.

"Whose idea was it to add pineapple to pizzas anyway?" Ethan asked.

"How did you get from banana milkshakes and sprinkles to that?" Emma asked with a laugh.

Ethan shrugged and blew his unruly hair from his eyes.

"It made sense to me."

"There's nothing wrong with pineapple on pizza," Luke said.

Ethan looked at him slack-jawed. "What have you done with Luke!?"

"I tried it over the summer. It was actually pretty good. We went to this awesome Italian place run by real Italians. My dad insisted on ordering a ham and pineapple pizza, and the chefs came out to shout at him. They said it was offensive to the name of pizza, and they didn't even stock pineapple. So, we went to this run down little place, and I gotta say, it was actually really good."

"Aw, come on, man. No way did that happen!" Ethan said.

"I don't know. I've heard Italians are really protective over their food," Emma shrugged.

They paused under a trio of streetlamps with droplet-shaped lights.

"You know, we could get pizza..." Alison began.

"No pineapple allowed!" Ethan added immediately.

"Luke *did* make it sound pretty good," Emma teased.

Ethan threw his hands up. "You're all experiments cooked up in a lab. Where are my real friends?"

Everyone laughed. The merriment died down as a small group of humans around their own age approached them. The leader, a tall narrow-shouldered guy with dyed black hair, didn't take his eyes off Alison.

"Remember us?" he asked, shoving his hands into the pockets of his tight pale blue jeans.

There was something familiar about them, but Alison couldn't quite put her finger on it.

"You're the ones who helped us out," Luke said quietly.

"Now it's time to return the favor," the boy said curtly.

"Excuse me?" Alison demanded.

She didn't like the pushy tone or the fact he just strolled up to them on the street. They were there to have a fun afternoon not be dragged into who knew what.

"We need to talk somewhere quiet..." the blonde human said.

"I don't like this," Emma whispered.

Alison agreed, and she instinctively began to draw on her magic in case they needed to defend themselves.

"Look, we helped you out before, and now, we're in a bit of trouble. We need a hand. It's *your* kind of trouble if you get my meaning."

"What did you do?" Ethan asked.

"We found something fun. We wanted to see what it was like to be one of you. It… didn't go like we expected."

Luke looked at his friends. Alison's mouth was pressed into a thin line. They knew they were going to be in deep trouble if they got caught being involved in illegal magic like this, but they did owe them.

"Show us," Alison finally said.

They followed the humans down a twisting path of alleys and finally emerged behind an abandoned building. The old wire fencing was rusty and peeled away from a well-used path. They ducked through the hole in the fence and passed yellowed grasses and scrubby little bushes. Alison saw the flickers of magic as they approached the back of the building. Small ribbons of pitch-black shadow curled and evaporated before forming a few inches away again.

"People are on their way. A neighbor complained about the noise. We need to deal with this now," the leader of the humans said.

Alison and her friends looked at the small, black wooden box that lay open on its side. The bare dirt had been painted a deep purple by the contents of the box.

"It was supposed to be some fun that would let us play with magic for an hour," a girl with a white and pink pixie cut confessed quietly.

The humans were all pressed back against the building as the darkness slowly spread and rumbled a short distance from the box. One of the girls was trembling, and Alison could see why. The magic felt malevolent. Luke growled as his wolf surged forward. His desire to protect his friends overriding his need to pretend he was human.

"Luke, keep the humans safe. Emma, help Ethan direct his magic. We'll envelope it in our own magic and crush it," Alison said with a confidence that she wasn't sure she felt.

Luke ushered the humans as far away from the darkness as possible. Emma and Ethan stood side-by-side looking at the black cloud as tendrils slowly stretched out as though tasting the air. Alison circled around it. When she got closer, she could feel pure violence rolling off it. Something within her told her that if they didn't squash it soon, then it would lose whatever bound it to the box, and then blood would be shed. She wasn't going to let that happen.

"We thought it was just some cool little puff of smoke at first, then Jacob went to touch it, and he screamed," the human leader admitted.

"We need to focus," Alison said.

They should have known that artifacts were illegal for a reason. They were often full of very dangerous magic that shouldn't be handled by humans. She pushed all that aside and allowed her Drow magic to suffuse her. They were going to need to work together to snuff out the magic.

She glanced at Emma who gave a small nod that Ethan echoed. Emma had been working hard on her magic, and she hoped it would be enough to help direct and guide Ethan's more erratic magic. He had talent, but he was still struggling to really get a grip on it.

Alison rolled her shoulders and slowly allowed her magic to slip out of her fingertips as she focused entirely on the black cloud before her. It was unlike anything she'd seen before. It looked as though it were draining the life and color from around it. Alison's magic combined with Ethan and Emma's magics forming a kaleidoscope of colors in her vision. It slowly wrapped around the dark cloud engulfing it. The darkness pressed back against her magic, and she felt chills running down her spine.

Emma was growing pale as their magic gradually compressed the cloud tighter.

"They'll be here soon. Hurry!" a female voice called.

Alison gritted her teeth. She pushed more of her magic into the effort, and suddenly the cloud was gone. Emma took a shaky breath, and Ethan put his arm around her shoulders.

They allowed their magic to slip away and were pleased to see there were no traces of whatever the malevolent thing was.

"Do not do that again," Alison snapped at the humans.

"Artifacts aren't something you screw around with for giggles," Luke growled.

"All right, lesson learned. You can't blame us. We want to be badasses, too," the human leader said.

"They're coming. We need to go!" the blonde girl said.

Alison and her friends took off after the humans running down the alleys not wanting to be there when the adults reached the site. They'd be in deep trouble if they were caught anywhere near an artifact like that. They parted ways with the humans and headed into the milkshake shop where they slumped down into the seats and let out loud laughs.

"It was an adventure," Luke said.

Emma shook her head and picked up one of the menus.

The shop really did have every flavor combination she could have imagined and far more. It was a quaint little shop with pretty, white tablecloths covered in delicate black patterns. Small hand-packed bags of cookies and cupcakes sat behind the tall wooden counter.

"They could have killed someone," Ethan murmured softly.

"Yeah, but we saved the day," Luke said, putting his menu back down.

"They got lucky," Alison clarified.

A bright and perky waitress with neatly styled hair and bright red lipstick came over to take their orders. To everyone's horror, Emma ordered the banana and Oreo milkshake. They all opted for more classic flavors to the waitress's disappointment.

Something about the incident was gnawing at Alison, but she couldn't quite figure out what it was. The wisps of thinner magic that had formed around the edge of the cloud reminded her a little of the odd magic she'd seen in Christie's magical aura. Of course, that couldn't have been connected, could it?

Alison was lost to her thoughts. Her mind skipped back to the missing books. There was something weird about that case too. She was going to get to the bottom of it all.

CHAPTER ELEVEN

They had managed to return to the school without any of the professors noticing, although Alison suspected that Horace knew. The groundskeeper had a small smirk on his face as he strolled across the front lawn. The evening passed without any more 'adventures'. Kathleen spent an hour talking about Professor Heineken, one of the newer professors at the school. Alison had learned that he taught about cars and magic, and he was from San Francisco.

"You know, I think we should start taking that class Alison. Cars are very useful after all."

Alison quirked an eyebrow and waited for the real reason Kathleen might show any interest in that particular class. She understood Peter's fascination, but Kathleen had no interest in getting her hands dirty.

"I've heard that he looks very good in those black overalls they make you wear when you look at the cars…"

Alison shook her head and smiled.

"I'm sure you can ask the headmistress about it if you're really that interested," she said.

Kathleen pulled her covers back and slipped into bed.

"I might just do that. I wonder if I can drop History."

"No, it's mandatory," Aya said quietly.

Kathleen huffed.

The girls slowly slipped into sleep while Alison lay awake watching the soul energies of her friends gradually take on pale blue hues as they relaxed and slept. She threw her covers back and quickly changed into jeans and a t-shirt and was surprised to see Aya doing the same.

"You don't mind if I join you, do you?"

"Of course not," Alison said, a feeling of relief washing over her.

Walking the grounds with Izzie had been relaxing and therapeutic, but doing it alone only added to the hole where Izzie should have been.

They padded through the school and stepped out into the cool, crisp night. The grass glistened under the moonlight where the heavy dew had fallen. It wouldn't be too long until the first frosts came.

"This is our senior year, and everything's different," Aya said, tucking her hands in the pockets of her hoodie.

They meandered across the open expanse of grass. The mountains seemed particularly close that evening Alison noted, and there was something about the way their broad peaks sat on the horizon.

"We have to apply for college soon, that's if we're even going. It feels like we're right on the cusp of something," Alison said softly.

Aya wove her arm around Alison's to remind her that

she wasn't alone. It could be a big scary world, and she had no doubt Alison was keenly aware of that.

"You're going to follow in your dad's footsteps?"

"Yeah. I'm going to become a bounty hunter. I want to do more than just catch bad guys though. I want to help both magicals and humans."

Alison felt as though there was a rift between the humans and magicals, and she wanted to do something to help heal that. The humans hadn't always been good to the magicals. There were certainly times of cruelty, but she wasn't going to let that color her views. They were people and individuals. Everyone deserved to feel safe and to know that there were people out there watching out for them.

"You're going to solve crimes and be a real badass?" Aya said nudging her playfully.

"Yes, exactly! First, I'm going to get to the bottom of those stolen books."

"They were just some history books, right? I'm sure it was just a prank."

"No, there's more to it than that. They were all connected, and they all have ties to transfiguration."

Aya frowned. "Do you think a human could be involved? They seemed pretty eager to play with magic in town earlier. They had no idea what they were dabbling with. I don't know what that thing was, but it could have killed a lot people if you hadn't shown up. What would they have done then?"

"And how much harm would it have done to the reputation of the school and magicals?" Alison said sadly.

"Exactly. Artifacts are dangerous for a reason, but they still blame us for making them in the first place."

Alison sighed, and their pace slowed a little.

"It feels like there's a huge weight hanging over the school, and I miss Izzie. What if she's not ok out there?"

"She kicks ass, and she has her parents with her. Don't worry. I'm sure she'll reappear and have the most amazing stories to tell."

Alison couldn't help but smile and hold onto that hope. Aya had to be right. She couldn't bear the possibility that her friend was hurt or worse.

"What do you know about that Christie girl you're practicing the musical with?"

Alison turned to look at her friend. Her tone had sounded suspicious.

"She's a freshman, and she talks a lot, but she's nice. Why?"

"I don't know. She seems friendly, but there's something a little weird about her. I swore I heard a clicking sound when I saw her yesterday. She had this look in her eye, a darkness. I blinked, and it was gone. It's probably just the stress getting to me. The classes are really hard this year."

Alison ran that through her mind. She didn't remember having seen any darkness in the girl. There was that odd spark though, but that hadn't been there when she'd seen her at their joint practice for the musical.

"What are you doing after this year?" Alison asked not hiding the fact she was changing the topic.

"I'm applying for college. I'm not sure what I want to do

yet, but I think having a degree to fall back on is a sensible idea. It gives me options."

Alison loved that Aya was so sensible and level headed.

"I haven't decided if I will go to college or not yet." Alison chewed on her bottom lip.

She wasn't sure how she'd cope going into a college without her friends around her. She knew she could handle herself with her magic and her fists if need be, but college was an entirely different thing. There would be all the strange looks and comments about her heritage. Everyone at the school knew her, and the whispers were mostly about the fight the previous semester which was far easier to shrug off. She had fought hard to keep her friends and fellow students safe. There was pride to be had in that.

Izzie had been more than her best friend; she had been Alison's rock and anchor, too.

"You'll be amazing no matter what you do. You excel at everything, and you kick ass, literally."

"Shay put me through my paces over the summer. She really upped my training. She really didn't hold back. She said if I wanted to follow in Brownstone's shoes, then I had to be prepared. You can't always depend on your magic."

"I think more people should be taught that. Our magic is a part of us, but it's not everything. I hate how divisive it is too."

Aya had never been very happy about the way that magic was often used to decide a person's social hierarchy. The shifters suffered because a lot of people didn't think their magic was real or counted. Luke had done well in school, but that had been by force of personality. How well would he do once he was outside of school among the larger society? He had a pack, but that still couldn't have been easy for him.

"I want to do something that helps smooth out those inequalities," Aya confessed.

"Like politics?"

Aya wrinkled her nose and looked appalled. "No. I'd sooner give up my magic than go into politics. I don't know how I'll do it yet, but I want to make the world a little better."

They found themselves headed to the barn where Horace and his aunt, Estelle were sitting on a bench in companionable silence. Horace's dog, a large golden retriever, was sprawled out at his feet. Estelle had a cigarette hanging from her lips but somehow managed to blow a string of perfect O's. Her bouffant was piled high on top of her head. Alison wasn't entirely sure how she did it. The woman must have spent hours on her hair every morning.

"Girls, what brings you out here tonight?" Horace asked amiably.

"We couldn't sleep," Aya said.

"You need to stop thinking so much and let your magic choose your path," Estelle said between puffs on her cigarette.

Alison looked at Aya hoping she had some insight. How was she supposed to let her magic choose her path?

"I'm going to be a bounty hunter." Alison lifted her chin.

"Don't force something. Your magic knows better than you. And you watch that Christie girl."

"Are you sure you mean Christie? The chatty freshman?"

"That's the one."

"Watch her? As in, be careful around her?" Aya asked.

Estelle didn't look at them. Instead, she blew another string of smoky O's. She'd said all she planned on saying about the topic. If the girls wanted to act on it, that was their business.

"It's getting late. You should be heading back to the dorm," Horace said, his dog stretching and yawning by his feet.

"Good night," the girls said before they turned and headed back to the school.

"Do you have any idea what that was all about?" Alison whispered, not wanting to offend the groundskeeper or his aunt.

"None. She saw something in Christie, too though."

Alison didn't understand what they possibly saw in Christie. She had seen nothing but kindness in the girl's soul. She was struggling to make friends and had no filter when she spoke, but there wasn't a bad bone in her body. Surely, she couldn't hide something like that from Alison's vision?

CHAPTER TWELVE

The days were passing quickly. The teenagers were taking off for another adventure. After all, it was their senior year.

Horace watched as Alison and her friends darted across the grass toward the car Ethan borrowed. He wasn't going to go and tell Mara about their escapades, but he was worried.

"Dorvu, do you want something new to do?"

The dragon looked up at him, intelligence and curiosity shining in his eyes.

"Follow Alison and her friends. Don't let the humans see you."

The dragon's mouth pulled into a sharp-toothed grin before he flapped his great silver wings and took off into the sky. He rode the cool air and followed behind the car in silence. He had been bored on the grounds. The rabbits were wise to his games, and he was too big to squeeze between the trees after the squirrels. The small game around the town would be more fun.

He followed the car down the road toward Charlottesville and remained high in the sky where the bright sun would hide him. His silvery scales shone in the bright light and made him look much like a painful sunbeam if anyone were to glance up at him.

The students piled out of the car near a park on the edge of town. He kept an eye on them as he circled, looking for rabbits or small birds to eat. His stomach growled as he swooped a little lower to see his future dinner better. No rabbits came into view, but there were some quails. Dorvu took one last look in the direction of the students and saw them laughing and joking as they walked down the street. Satisfied they were safe enough he flew down closer to the longish grass and flushed the birds out.

They took off into the sky with startled cries, and one flew right in front of the dragon's nose. He opened his mouth and swallowed it in one bite. To his delight, the other birds lacked the intelligence to go far. They fluttered around his vicinity in a panic, and he plucked them out of the sky.

Tanner put his arm around Alison's waist, and she leaned into him glad of his presence. Emma and Luke were discussing the details of a Louper game they'd seen.

"He just fell into the abyss!"

"He was too focused on his tracker and wasn't paying any attention." Emma shook her head.

"Not being able to lean entirely on magic has some advantages."

"Knowing how to use your skills and understanding your limits will always win," Tanner said.

Luke rolled his eyes.

"Remind me again who's team captain," Luke said, puffing up his chest a little but unable to keep the grin off his face.

"I was helping you out. Magic isn't everything." He laughed and added, "It's the only thing."

Alison laughed at the mock horror on Luke's face. Everyone knew Luke had worked every spare hour training to make sure he could be the captain. Not having magic wasn't slowing him down.

"Afternoon," the human from their last visit said gruffly.

He was flanked by a trio of other humans, each with dyed hair and heavily done make-up.

"Who gave you that black eye?" Luke asked.

Confusion spread across the black-haired boy's face.

"It's eye-liner…"

"Why on Earth would a guy be wearing eye-liner?"

"I think they call it guy-liner," Tanner mused.

"Look, thanks for the other day. You want to grab a coffee?"

The magicals looked at each other. Luke shrugged. "Sure."

"Why don't we go to Mel's?" The girl with the white pixie cut with pink streaks asked.

"How have things been since we were last here?" Luke asked.

"About the same. I'm Chase, by the way," the leader said, extending his hand.

"Luke." He gestured to his friends, "Emma, Ethan, Alison, and Tanner."

"That's Lydia." He pointed to the girl with the pixie cut. "Ben," the scrawny blonde boy with scruffy hair, "and Mags," the girl with long dark blonde hair tied back in a French braid.

"So, are you ditching school or?"

"I wouldn't call it ditching…" Luke put his hands in the pockets of his jeans.

They'd finished their classes for the day and just needed a bit of freedom. It felt oppressive at the school sometimes.

"You just wanted to hang out with the normals," Lydia said wryly.

Alison looked at her trying to decide if that was a dig or not. Was that how they viewed themselves, as the normal ones? Their magic was perfectly normal, but she'd seen enough human media to know that they were distrustful of the magical. Some saw them as dangerous freaks, while others bowed to them desperately wanting magic of their own.

"We wanted some time to hang out and relax without teachers watching over our shoulders," Tanner said.

Mel's cafe was a small building with a concrete patio in front of it surrounded by a loosely hung chain to mark its boundaries. The simple, square tables were made from dark painted wood with big blue umbrellas in the middle for those warmer days. The structure itself reminded Alison of a barn with its gently sloping roof and big glass frontage. The smells coming from inside were rich coffee and greasy food that made Luke's mouth water.

They took a patio table near the alley away from prying ears. The air chilled for a moment when Dorvu flew nearby making sure they weren't getting involved in something dangerous. Not that anyone noticed him, they just huddled a little closer and assumed the breeze was due to the time of year.

Everyone ordered coffee, and finally, Chase spoke.

"What's it like? Being magical? I mean… everyone says only the bad guys have magic. There was a big crime committed by some wizard yesterday. He broke into a jeweler's and stole this big ass diamond. They say he froze the glass and smashed through it. The employees have hypothermia and are in the hospital."

Alison wondered if Brownstone was hunting the wizard down right then. She was going to stop those sorts of people and stop humans and magicals alike from getting hurt.

"It's hard to describe. Is that really what you think of us all? Of magicals?" Emma asked quietly.

The other customers sitting outside were far too engrossed in their food and conversation to worry about the students.

"You have powers to control the elements and summon things. You change the world around you. You have freakin' magic," Mags said.

The blonde leaned closer, looking at the magicals. They looked normal to her. Well, the girl with mostly white hair stood out a bit. There was something a bit weird about her, but the hair could have been dyed. How many other magicals were just walking down the street without them even realising? Were they dangerous?

"And we understand that magic isn't something to be used to harm others. We protect people. We try to make the world a bit better," Alison said.

She hated that she was seen as some villain. Of course, there were bad people out there, and those who used their magic for harm. That could be said of anything though.

"So, like, what are you?" Chase asked.

The magicals looked at each other. It was very rude to ask such a question. Did they really want to explain what they were? Emma was fascinated by the views of these humans.

"Is everyone like you? Do you want magic? That's why you took the artifact, right?"

Chase took a big gulp of his coffee, and Lydia paled at the mention of the artifact.

"That was just a stupid mistake. You can't blame us though. Magic looks so cool. It's like something from the comics. Our parents say that magicals are just freaks who can't be trusted though. They say that you're all just biding your time before you take over the world and make us your slaves or something. Do you do big blood sacrifices?"

Alison's mouth fell open at Mag's question. The very idea of making a blood sacrifice appalled her. She would never take someone's life like that.

"No. Why would we do blood sacrifices? Is that on the news too? Our magic comes..." Tanner stopped, unsure how much he should say.

"There was some gruesome murder last month. A couple was found in the woods with their throats slashed, and some symbol painted in their blood on the tree they were tied to," Chase said.

"Did they catch who did it?" Alison asked.

"Not yet. Some people think it was a magical. Others think it was a human trying to become one of you. There are lots of those you know. I think some of them are pretty crazy and would do anything to have a taste of your magic," Ben said.

And that was why artifacts were illegal. They were dangerous and even more so in the hands of someone who had no idea what they were doing. But in the hands of someone who had no intention of using the magic for the good of others, it would be far too easy to cause chaos and pain.

CHAPTER THIRTEEN

A friendly Louper game between the seniors and the alumni had been arranged on the clear winter day. The skies were bright, pale blue, and the stands were packed. The fairies had come out in high numbers eager to see how the teams fared against each other. Their translucent wings fluttered in the bright sunlight as they waited for the teams to take the field.

Alison and her friends had arrived early to get the best seats with an unobstructed view of the entire field. Ethan and Luke were confident that they could win against the alumni. They'd been training hard all summer and had a strong team around them. A hush fell over the field when the two teams jogged onto the field. The seniors took their place at the northern end of the field, with the alumni in the south.

Luke couldn't keep the grin off his face. He was sure he was going to kick the alumni's asses. He knew how his former teammates worked and planned on using that to his advantage.

"Remember, they might be older, but we're smarter and faster," Luke told the team around him.

"They're going to underestimate us," Ethan said.

"And we're going to make the most of that. Everyone ready?"

Luke looked around at the eager faces. Each of them was at their peak. They'd been training hard and had really come together as a team.

The field disappeared and was replaced with a dark, foreboding forest surrounding a small hill with the ruins of a castle at the top. A thick fog rolled over the thin grass and wove its way between the heavy boughs of the trees, sending a shiver down the players' spines. The canopy had fallen for the year leaving the pale grey sky overhead exposed. It felt as though something dark had swallowed the color around them leaving a dull grey landscape.

The alumni spread out in a small circle and tried to get a feel for their new surroundings. They had more magic between them than the seniors which gave them a broader scope of abilities to tackle challenges. David formed a set of pale white orbs to provide more light while they decided which way to go.

"The castle seems the most reasonable," Wyatt said.

Something made the broad oak tree nearest them shiver. Its great limbs shook and trembled in the cool, damp air. The team looked around trying to find the source of the movement. The other trees were still.

The crowd in the stands gasped as a black-headed serpent burst out from the heart of the tree and dove straight at David. The Light Elf dove to the side and rolled away just as the beast's long, curved fangs went to close around him. Wyatt and Sean moved to either side of the snake and formed shards of brilliant white magic. They plunged the magic deep into the thick hide of the snake, and it disintegrated in a small cloud of blue smoke.

"I hate snakes," David ground out.

The spectators cheered and whooped, pleased to see the alumni tackled their first challenge with speed and finesse. The seniors were already advancing up the hill toward the castle. They jogged through the trees and remained in a close-knit group as the fog closed in around them, and the sense that something was watching them filled the air. Silence descended as the spectators saw a pair of hounds creeping through the fog toward the group of seniors. Their rough pelts bristled as they bared long, yellowed teeth, and their eyes flashed red.

Luke's ears pricked. His shifter senses were screaming at him to get out of there, and fast.

"Come on, get moving!" he shouted.

Rex yelped as something sank into his lower leg, and he was back on the field. The crowd was torn between cheering and quiet dismay. The seniors stopped dead and closed ranks as they looked around for what had taken Rex. Luke heard it first and growled deep in his throat. He trusted his instincts and leapt into the fog, landing on one of the hound's back. It vanished without so much as a sound.

Ethan saw the second hound emerge out of the fog and took a deep breath. The hound bared its teeth at him; its hackles rose, making it appear even larger. Its shoulder came almost halfway up Ethan's ribs, and its mouth was large enough to wrap around his thigh. Ethan hesitated a moment before he formed a magical net and wrapped it around the hound's head, removing the threat of its teeth. Dan took the chance to tackle it to the ground as Luke returned.

The crowd burst into jubilant applause. The alumni were equally as far up the hill as the seniors now. The castle loomed above them. The teams didn't see the gargoyles circling above with sharp claws ready to plunge into whoever dared enter their domain.

Henry's blond hair fell into his eyes as they crested the ridge and got their first look at the castle. He tried to tuck his hair behind his ear out of the way, but it refused to stay put. Something about the castle bugged him. His shifter instincts told him to stay away.

"There's something bad in there," he murmured.

Wyatt looked at his best friend with a raised eyebrow.

"A monster?"

"Not sure. I just know I don't want to go in there."

"That'll be where the disk is then, and we can't let those seniors win."

Henry kept his body low and stuck close to the trees as they approached the towering remains of the castle. A broad wall with small slit windows was directly in front of them. The crumbled remains of another wall butted up against it where it would have formed a corner once. A sound caught his attention. His ears pricked, and he listened more closely, grabbing onto the back of David's shirt to stop him from stepping into the castle.

"Gargoyles. Four or five of them," Henry whispered.

Everyone looked skyward trying to spot them. A screech cut through the air, and David's breath caught in his throat. Five gargoyles came out of nowhere and were hurtling toward them. They hid behind the wall and called on their magic. He formed a set of small throwing knives and leaned out around the wall trying to spot their attackers. He threw a knife, aiming for the heart of the closest gargoyle flying back and forth between the walls. He missed and drew the gargoyle's attention.

"Well done," Wyatt hissed.

David ignored him as he called on his magic once again to try a different approach. Henry flattened himself against the wall just before Wyatt summoned a small wall of fire. Sweat beaded on his forehead as he fought to control the flames. The gargoyles screamed and evaporated.

The seniors heard the screams and paused looking around for the source. When nothing came for them, they scrambled through the ragged hole in the stone wall and emerged in a small room with a pale blue brick floor. A thin layer of dark green moss covered most of the bricks giving it a patchy appearance.

Luke crouched and looked at the bricks, something about them seemed wrong. Ethan cautiously reached out his foot and tapped one. It crumbled down into an inky black abyss.

"Looks like we're trying a different route," he observed.

"No," Shannon said.

She held her arm out blocking the way back through the window as she called up her magic. Slowing her breathing, she reached into the moss with her magic and pressed against it looking for the safe route. She smiled triumphantly when a neon yellow path formed.

"Follow the yellow brick road."

Ethan rolled his eyes, but Luke patted her on the back.

"Well done. Come on, get going." He stepped onto the first yellow brick and found it held.

They rushed across the room and crept into what could have been the feast hall. It was a large rectangular room with a fireplace taller than Luke on the eastern wall. The dark grey stone was still marked by black soot. Well-worn corners dipped in a simple braided pattern that would have been quite striking when it was new. Old flaking wood remained within the wide grate where the last fire had been burned. There was something a little sad about the disrepair it now sat in.

Alison watched unable to look away as the alumni charged through the former kitchen of the castle and took the steep staircase down into the basement, or perhaps dungeon. Darkness wrapped around them, forcing them to slow their pace. A rhythmic dripping of water cut through the oppressive quiet of the place. Henry paused and listened while Wyatt and David pushed on, sure that the seniors were closing in. The gold disk had to be close by; they were sure of it.

"In the corner!" Henry shouted.

"What? An enemy? What's in the corner?" David asked.

"The disk, I can feel it."

They surged forward, feet slipping on the slimy floor. Henry pushed past his friends and took point, making the most of his superior vision while Wyatt tried to form a light to guide the rest of them. His yellow orb faltered and flickered out three times before David finally summoned one.

The shadows receded into the corners revealing a low-ceilinged room with wide, heavy stone slabs on the floor coated in grimy, reddish slime. They trod carefully, trying not to lose their balance as they approached a small wooden chest.

"It's in there. I'm sure of it," Henry said.

Excitement filled the shifter as he closed in on the chest. They heard the seniors' footsteps above them where they must have been going through the kitchen. A clang of metal on stone came before a shout of surprise.

The remaining pots and pans flew off the hooks toward the seniors' heads.

"Run!" Luke shouted and dove down toward the stairs into the gloom.

"They're right behind us!" Wyatt urged.

Henry took the risk and ran forward, lunging at the chest. He tried to wrench it open only to find it wouldn't budge. Had he been wrong?

His friends crowded around him, and David took the chest from him, inspecting it while the seniors cautiously made their way down the stairs.

Alison saw the faint glow of magic around the chest. She knew they needed to press the small lion head at the top of the chest, but the guys were trying to fumble with the lock instead. She silently urged her friends on. If they could get the chest out of the alumni team's hands, she was sure Luke would know what to do.

Then Wyatt spotted it and jabbed the lion head. The lid sprang open and revealed the gold disk. He reached inside and held it up triumphantly. The crowd exploded in cheers and a standing ovation as they called out the alumni team's names.

Alison couldn't help but be a little disappointed, but it was a fantastic game, and she cheered for the winners. They'd worked hard and won fairly. The seniors' saw just how close they had been and smiled as they congratulated the winners. They'd do better next time.

Wyatt, Henry, and David pulled their former teammates into a friendly hug.

"You guys did great. You're going to kick ass in the big tournament. Make us proud," Wyatt said.

Luke and Ethan both beamed with pride. They'd worked hard, and it felt good to have that recognized and praised.

"Don't worry. We'll win next time," Ethan said with a wink.

CHAPTER FOURTEEN

The room Alison shared with her friends positively buzzed as they started to get ready for the Homecoming dance. Kathleen finally emerged from the bathroom and admired the emerald green flapper dress she had picked out for the occasion. The glittery layers sparkled under the lights and would move much like feathers when she put it on.

"Don't forget Christie's coming to get ready with us," Alison reminded them as she dried her hair and perched on the edge of her bed.

The younger girl still wasn't getting along all that well with the girls she roomed with, so Alison had invited her to come and get ready with her. Emma chewed on her bottom lip as she held up her sapphire silk dress. "Are you sure it isn't too short?"

"With your legs, you could easily go a few inches shorter," Kathleen reassured her.

"You'll look stunning," Aya said as she dashed into the bathroom before someone else could claim it.

Christie knocked on the door and tried to still her hands. Homecoming was an alien thing to her. They didn't have it in England. She'd picked out what she thought was a pretty dress, and she'd spent ages choosing her accessories for it. She rolled a small, silver pot engraved with runes back and forth in her hand while she waited for someone to open the door. Had she gotten the room number wrong?

Emma opened the door with a flourish, "Come in, come in." she ushered Christie.

"Is that your dress?" Kathleen pointed at the silvery swath of fabric over Christie's arm.

"Yes. Did I get it wrong? They said the theme was a masquerade ball on Bourbon street, which was kinda hard to research. I mean, New Orleans has such a huge culture to it, and a masquerade ball is a specific thing."

Kathleen's mouth quirked into a smile, and she put her arm around Christie's shoulders and guided her to her bed.

"Show us. I'm sure it'll be beautiful."

Everyone paused to look as Christie unfolded her dress and revealed a confection of light fabrics in soft silvers and whites. It had an ethereal look to it.

Kathleen ran her fingers over the delicate fabric. "It's stunning. I wish I'd found it first."

"Oh, I'm sure your dress is just perfect," Christie reassured her.

Kathleen beamed.

"It is. It highlights my best features." She held up her emerald dress, and Christie admired the sleek lines.

"What's that? In your hand," Alison asked.

"Oh! It's something I made. I found a potions book, and

there was a recipe for a paste that will make our hair look like natural wonders."

Emma and Aya looked at each other not sure they liked the sound of that.

"I'll show you," Christie said, laying her dress down on Kathleen's bed.

She unscrewed the silver lid and dipped her fingers into the clear paste then ran it over a section of hair around her face. To the girls' amazement, her hair started to shine like spun gold. When she moved, it shimmered with every shade of blonde and looked like the sun was drenching it.

"You made that?" Kathleen asked.

"Yes, it wasn't that hard, not really. A couple of the ingredients were difficult to source, but I managed to sneak them onto the school grounds. Trying to get into the lab after hours was the hardest part really. Would you like some?"

"Once I've done my make-up."

No one could keep the smiles off their faces as they changed into their dresses and started weaving their magic to form their masks and make-up.

"This is Bourbon Street, so we need flashes of color to really shine," Kathleen announced as she held Aya's chin steady.

Aya closed her eyes as Kathleen called upon her magic and gently brushed it over Aya's cheekbones and around her eyes. Slowly a delicate mask began to form. It was constructed of thin silvery threads and looked like it had been woven from pure moonlight. The mask framed Aya's eyes and high-lighted her sharp cheekbones. When she opened her eyes, they looked like rich honey in contrast to the pale silver. Combined with her short crimson dress, she looked like a whole new girl from the quiet one everyone knew and loved.

Christie finished it off with her paste that made Aya's dark hair iridescent like a crow's wing. It developed rich bottle green and ocean blue sheens as she turned her head, and it caught the light.

The girls bustled around helping each other refine their make-up and add the magical touches that made every-thing that little bit more beautiful. Alison added a thin layer of shadow magic to her short form-fitting black dress, and Emma used her magic to weave Alison's hair into an elegant updo complete with fluttering butterflies. Christie's paste gave her hair the appearance of freshly fallen snow; it glistened and glittered.

Kathleen, not one to be up-staged, added magically woven feathers to her red hair. They gradually turned color, shifting through bold reds into fiery oranges and finally jewel blues before starting back at red. Everyone crowded around Christie in her stunning silvery dress and helped her form a twisting knotwork mask. They stood back and admired their work as the younger girl stood with her sun-drenched hair and beautiful silver dress and mask. She couldn't keep the broad smile from her face as everyone looked pleased with their work.

"You need one last thing," Kathleen declared.

She pulled out a delicate silver bracelet formed from tiny feathers and put it on Christie's wrist.

"It's the perfect final piece."

Christie looked down at the bracelet and fought back her tears of happiness. They had all been so kind to her, and it was overwhelming her. The girls pulled her into a hug.

"Tonight is for happiness, so no tears allowed," Alison said firmly.

Christie nodded and took a deep breath, fighting back the tears before it could smudge her mascara. A knock came from the door. "The boys are here!" Kathleen called.

Alison ran her hands over her dress and smoothed out non-existent wrinkles. She wanted to be perfect for Tanner. Kathleen opened the door and ushered Tanner, Luke, and Hunter, Kathleen's date into the room.

"We're seniors, we can bend the 'no boys' rule just this once."

Tanner stopped dead in his tracks and admired his girl-friend. She was a vision to behold. He tried to commit every detail into his memory. He was positive she was the most beautiful woman he had ever laid eyes on. Alison went to him and kissed him tenderly. He had put a smart black blazer and white shirt with his best blue jeans.

"You look incredible," Tanner whispered, not wanting the moment to end.

Alison cupped his cheek and looked into his eyes, watching the familiar colors of his soul. She saw the adoration there, the full glow of his affection for her.

"Come on. You can't stare into each other's eyes all night!" Kathleen said.

She had hooked her arm around Hunter's, a broad-shouldered half elf that she had asked to the dance a few days prior. Luke was a little quiet because he missed Izzie, but he kept a smile on his face and focused on the joy of his friends. It was a night of fun and celebrations.

Emma and Aya put their arms around Christie's and guided her out of the room.

"Don't worry. We'll be your dates for the night," Aya said.

Christie grinned feeling as though she finally had a place. Everyone had been so kind to her that it was a relief after a difficult few weeks.

***

The rich, soulful sound of a saxophone spread throughout the corridors. Tanner kept his arm around Alison's waist as they followed Kathleen and her date into the hall. All heads turned as they walked in, much to Kathleen's delight. Conversations and dancing quickly resumed as everyone's curiosity had been sated.

Tanner led Alison to a quiet corner where she could stand and admire the decorations around them. The plain walls now had bold blocks of color from bright pinks to spearmint greens and vivid yellows. Each had intricately painted balconies forming three stories. Orange and black lanterns hung from invisible threads of magic between bright green ferns overflowing their simple wooden baskets. Tall palm trees sprouted from planters around the room, and familiar street signs stood at even intervals.

A thin, gauzy white fabric hung above the ferns and lanterns giving everything a more intimate feeling. The jazz music had been magically enhanced to reverberate around the room and make it feel as though the small band was playing near each and every student. The band was dressed in simple suits and closed their eyes as they lost themselves to the music. The pianist, a wizard with wild black hair that refused to be tamed, had a look of utter bliss on his face as his fingers danced across the keys.

The students danced to the increasing tempo of the music, and Tanner took Alison's hand once she had taken in all the details. They made their way onto the main dance floor and danced with their bodies close and Alison's head on Tanner's shoulder. The music pulsed through them and carried them away to a carefree place filled with the rich sound of laughter and the heady scents of ocean air and thick, rich vanilla.

Christie, Aya, and Emma danced together with grins on their faces as the stress and tension of the recent week slipped away into oblivion. The girls received many admiring glances, but they were far more interested in their own company than that of the guys.

Kathleen made sure to dance with her tall, strong date in the very center of the dance floor where everyone could see them. She didn't miss the expressions of envy that passed over a few of the girl's faces. Hunter put his arms around her waist and held her close, and she allowed him. She didn't think she'd see him again after the dance, but she was going to enjoy the night. Alison and Tanner were looking at each other with absolute bliss, entirely lost to their own little world, and Kathleen found herself smiling. They were the perfect couple, and she hoped she found her own Tanner when she was ready.

"We should get some punch," Christie said over the increasingly excited jazz music.

The dance floor was growing crowded, and everyone was feeling swept away by the strong beat and rhythm of the music. It told a tale of love, passion, and long sultry nights.

Christie, Emma, and Aya wove through the crowds and headed to the small table fashioned like a bar complete with a pair of bartenders in white shirts and black suspenders.

"And what can I get you, fine ladies?"

"Red punch, please," Emma said.

"Same," Aya and Christie echoed.

The bartender poured a cherry red punch into an elegant highball glass. He dropped a candied glace cherry into Emma's glass and winked. She smiled and looked away before she took her drink. The girls wandered over to the only spare table around the edge of the room. The table cloth was a simple black affair that helped it blend into the shadows of the corners where the girls could sit down and have a little quiet time.

Christie took a sip of her punch and found it to be an interesting mix of tart cranberry, sour cherry, and sweet almost bubble gum. She wouldn't have put those flavors together, and it fizzed on her tongue. She took a proper drink, enjoying it far more than she expected.

"Is Kathleen hoping to be Homecoming queen?" Christie asked.

"Yes, but she's up against Aimee. Do you know Aimee? She's the beautiful Light Elf whom everyone adores," Aya said.

"Everyone but you," Christie observed.

Aya shrugged. "I think she's shallow, but it doesn't matter. The Homecoming queen thing won't have any effect on real life stuff. Let her have her moment, you know?"

Christie looked over at Alison and Tanner and thought they would make the perfect Homecoming couple. They were perfect together, and the way they looked at each other was straight out of a romance movie.

"What do you think of your first homecoming?" Emma asked.

"It's amazing! Everyone looks so beautiful, and the decorations are incredible! My school in London didn't have homecoming, and if there was a dance, we just put up a few balloons and called it good. They never did anything like this. The buildings almost look real, and the lanterns really add to the atmosphere. I feel like I'm at the most amazing street party in New Orleans! I've never been to New Orleans, but I picture it feeling like this. They even have the smell of the sea!"

The girl's enthusiasm was infectious. *She should have more friends, and what is it about her that's off*, thought Aya. Christie never had a bad thing to say about anyone, and she was always so bubbly and happy. It was fun being around her, but still.

Once the dance had wound down for the night, and the group was sitting on the benches in front of the school, Luke disappeared into the night. Alison curled up with her head on Tanner's shoulder and enjoyed the comfortable silence. They all stood and started to head back inside when the temperature began to drop. Tanner put his jacket over Alison's bare shoulders and gently held her close.

A howl cut through the silence of the evening. Quickly

followed by answering howls. Luke was out running with his pack.

Breakfast was a little later than usual to help the students and teachers cope with the late night before. Luke had forgone his usual omelette in favor of eggs over medium with extra bacon.

"Good run? You didn't get in until sunrise," Tanner said.

"Yeah," Luke said, shoving a piece of bacon in his mouth.

"I'm glad to see manners haven't entirely died out amongst shifters," Kathleen teased.

Luke looked at her as he stuffed another slice of bacon into his mouth and smiled. Kathleen rolled her eyes.

"Can you believe Aimee won Homecoming queen?" Kathleen sniffed.

Aya and Emma looked at each other before they said in unison, "yes."

Alison and Tanner laughed when Kathleen scowled and picked at her eggs.

"It's just a silly popularity contest, you know," Ethan said.

"Who was that blonde girl with you last night?" Peter asked.

"Christie, she's playing Madame Morrible in the musical. I told you about her," Alison said.

Peter frowned and tried to recall any mention of a Madame Morrible or the musical. None of it rang any bells. He'd been far too busy trying to form small magical automatons. He was currently using iron filings to form the body, so they could be disassembled and reassembled quickly and easily. The magic wasn't quite coming together, and they fell over when they tried to walk. They were only a few inches tall, but he was sure he could make something full human size. They would be very useful for factory work, or perhaps military and science too.

"Peter? I asked if you did the portals homework," Emma said, nudging him in the ribs.

He looked at her bewildered.

"There was portals homework?"

Aya handed him a page of notes. "If you're quick, you can work from mine."

"You're the best!"

He pushed his plate aside and scribbled down what he thought he was supposed to be writing. Aya had written something about the delicate nature of portals and the long-term maintenance of them. It sounded sort of familiar, but he hadn't been paying attention in portals class. It wasn't entirely relevant to his future business plans.

They rushed to portals class and sat in their usual seats while Professor Cooper watched them. His short salt and pepper beard looked like it had gained a few more white hairs since Peter had joined his class. Satisfied that everyone was where they were supposed to be, he asked everyone to hand in their homework. He wasn't at all surprised to see that the ink was almost still wet on Peter's. He let it slide as he was a good student. He just needed a firm hand.

"Did you see the dress that Zoe wore?" the part-witch in front of Alison said to her friend.

"Yes, it was hand-crafted from a mix of fairy and witch magic. How did she afford that?"

"Seriously? I didn't think the fairies allowed their magic anywhere near the likes of us," Kathleen chimed in.

"That's what I heard. Alison, did you see the magic on Zoe's dress?"

The girls turned around to face Alison expectantly, entirely ignoring the weary look on Professor Cooper's face. He would allow them to gossip for a few minutes. Homecoming was very important to the students after all.

"Yes. It was beautifully constructed. It did look like there was some fairy magic in there, but it was mostly witch magic."

"So, it's true! I need to know where she got it from," the part-witch said.

"All right, that's quite enough. Today, we're going to be looking at the different characteristics of short distance vs. long distance portals, and the roles they play within our world."

Alison tried to pay attention. Portals didn't particularly interest her, but they might come in useful during her time as a bounty hunter.

CHAPTER FIFTEEN

Alison heard an odd clicking sound as Christie left the classroom. They had been practicing their parts for the musical. Christie's magic contained the slate grey smudge near the crown of her head again. Alison hadn't seen the smudge for a while and had assumed that it was a remnant from an earlier class, but they had come from dinner this time though.

When asked about it, Christie had looked slightly alarmed and Alison caught the soft shimmer of a lie but felt it was best not to push her too hard. It was likely that the other girl had simply been trying to practice her magic to keep up in her classes.

"Did you hear? More books went missing!"

Alison paused and tried to see who had said that. A trio of juniors walked past her whispering about books.

"Straight from Professor Powell's own collection I heard!"

Alison still hadn't figured out who had taken the history of transfiguration books or how they did it. She wasn't going to let this drop. She made her way through the corridors toward Professor Powell's office. It was late, but he was known for keeping odd hours. She knocked on the dark wooden door and waited. There was a reasonable chance that he would send her away, but this was her first chance to try out her bounty hunting skills, and she wasn't going to let it drop that easily.

Professor Powell opened the door and frowned down at Alison.

"Can I help you?"

"Is it true that books have been taken from your office?" There was no point in beating around the bush.

He narrowed his eyes. "Has word spread that quickly?"

"I'm afraid so. So, it's true?"

He sighed and glanced back at the packed bookshelves in his office. It was true, and he was at a loss as to how they had done it. His office was heavily warded and locked when he wasn't in it. His personal collection of books contained many tomes that were entirely unsuitable for students. He didn't practice dark magic any more, but that didn't mean that he had stopped studying it. There could be a time when he needed such knowledge.

Alison stood with her shoulders back and a look of pure determination on her face. Professor Powell understood that she wouldn't be budging an inch until she got the information she had come for. If he remembered correctly, her adopted father was a renowned bounty hunter, and she planned on following in his footsteps.

"Come inside, Miss Brownstone."

He stepped aside and gestured her into his office. The wooden floor was gently scuffed, and his desk had a few pockmarks from where his temper had gotten the better of him. The back wall was floor to ceiling bookshelves packed full of leather-bound books. His collection contained everything relating to dark magic, a little on portals, history, and the delicate art of transfiguration.

Xander closed the door with a soft click.

"The thief took three books. Each of which was on the topic of transfiguration. One was on the hypothetical concept of changing one magical type with another. It was merely a thought experiment."

"The other books tied into transfiguration too. The thief clearly planned on transfiguring something and potentially a person."

Xander looked at the small gap on his shelf. He didn't understand how the thief had managed to not only take the books but do so undetected. The gnomes had already tried their spells to retrieve it, and they had failed.

"What exactly did the books cover?" asked Alison.

"As I said, one was a thought experiment on the idea of changing a person's make-up and magic. The other two were on the intricacies of transfiguration."

Alison thought about it and tried to understand what the person intended, and perhaps more importantly, *how* they were doing it.

Mara burst into the office startling Alison.

"They took two books from my private quarters," Mara said before she noticed Alison.

The headmistress composed herself and looked at Alison.

"Can you please tell me what books were taken? I'm going to find the thief."

She spoke with such confidence. There was no room for doubt that she was sure she was going to catch this thief despite the fact the teachers around her couldn't.

"They were two books on the intricate make-up and nature of a person's magic. They detailed the theories on how our magic is woven into our beings, and the effects it has upon us."

"Would you mind if I looked at where they were taken from?"

Alison knew she was pushing her luck, but if the books had just been taken, there could be some faint trail of magic. Mara pressed her lips together and looked at Xander who shrugged. The young Drow had shown herself to be dedicated and talented. Mara relented and led her to her private quarters.

Alison looked around the spacious area full of light and warmth. There were small touches of slate grey magic where the books had been, and she could make out a faint trail leading to the door, but it stopped dead at the threshold of Mara's quarters. Alison sighed in frustration. Someone was stealing books to do with transformation. She was increasingly sure that they wanted to change their own or someone else's magical type, but she still had no idea who it was or how they were doing it.

The following day the friends went down to the kemana to do some early Christmas shopping. Emma had invited Christie along because she'd never been before. She'd gotten a rare freshman pass for her from the headmistress.

Christie looked around with wide eyes and absolute awe on her face. The colors were stunning as they stepped out into the market proper. Each stall was unique and entirely individual.

"Further back there are more established shops. Is there anything, in particular, you'd like to see?" Alison asked.

"I have no idea," Christie said, feeling overwhelmed.

"We'll split up so that we can get gifts for each other," Kathleen declared.

Emma hooked her arm around Christie's. "Come on. We'll show you around. I'm sure you'll find plenty of wonderful things."

Aya went with Emma and Christie as they headed to the north. They walked at a slow, casual pace, allowing Christie plenty of time to look at everything around her. Magic clung to every surface. They paused to look over a small selection of silver jewelry, hand-crafted by a young witch with aquamarine hair. She painted a big smile on her face as she watched the students closely. They were unlikely to be able to afford her wares, but they could have rich parents.

Emma leaned a little closer, looking at a delicate chain bracelet. Three loops of finely woven chain came together at a small rune disk. She didn't recognize the symbol.

"What does this do?"

The witch picked it up off the black velvet and prepared her sales pitch.

"This brings a little luck and excitement to the wearer. It's a beautiful piece isn't it, simple enough for everyday but elegant enough to dress up with too. I crafted it and imbued the magic myself, so I can guarantee it works."

"What do you mean by 'brings excitement to the wearer'?"

Emma narrowed her eyes a little at the bracelet, that sounded like a chaos type of spell. It was all very good on paper, but that could become dangerous if you weren't careful.

"Just what I said. It brings excitement," the witch said tightly.

The girls looked at each other and moved on. They didn't want to risk something like that bringing trouble into their lives.

Alison walked with Kathleen in companionable silence as they made their way past crystal shops and paused to take in the beautiful artwork made by a Light Elf. The landscapes were so vivid Alison felt as though she could put her hand right into them.

"I thought we could get Ethan some focusing bands. Something simple and trendy so no one knows what they are. He's going to college, and a little help with controlling his magic would probably be best for everyone," Kathleen said as she squeezed around a group of gossiping wood elves.

"He hasn't blown anything up in weeks." Alison laughed.

"Oh well, that's sorted it then, he's clearly perfect!" Kathleen threw her hands up, laughing too.

"He tries really hard."

"I know, and I want to help him, really I do. Do you think he'll take them the wrong way?"

Alison frowned and looked over a set of wands.

"No. I think they're a great idea," she finally said.

"He'd lose or break a wand in no time," Kathleen said, tugging her friend away from the slender pieces of wood and crystal. "He's already broken a few."

They made their way through the organized chaos toward the magical aids shop. Kathleen walked into the brightly lit space with a purpose that caught the shop owner's eye. He watched them warily, knowing people like that were either the best customers of the day or the worst. He hoped she wasn't going to be demanding and fussy.

Kathleen paused in the middle of the room and turned a slow circle looking for the focusing bands. There were wands, stones and crystals, and a variety of pendants in every shape and color. Alison gestured toward the display of bands in the corner closest to the counter.

"We want something classy and simple," Kathleen said.

"Oh, these are so very Ethan," Alison said, picking up a set of thick gold chain bracelets.

Kathleen looked absolutely aghast at their very existence before Alison laughed and put them down.

They edged along the display, moving away from the beads and chains to the leather bands. The wider bands with metal inserts didn't seem very Ethan to Alison. She pointed at a trio of slender leather bands joined by a small silver piece.

"What about those? He could call those a fashion statement, and they'd fit with his usual aesthetic."

"Scruffy and unkempt," Kathleen finished.

"He's gotten much better. He tried to iron his shirt last week."

Kathleen snorted. Ethan was a good friend, but he

always looked as though he'd rolled out of bed and fallen into his clothes.

"Why don't we talk to the others, and we can gather our funds and get these?" Kathleen pointed to four slender, braided leather bracelets with small black gems joining them.

"They are our most potent focusing bands," the shop-keeper said.

"I think they're perfect," Alison said.

Tanner frowned and looked around, trying to figure out where on Earth he'd gone wrong. He swore that he needed to take two lefts, a right, and then straight for two sections. Yet where he thought there was supposed to be a book store, there was a food stall selling fairy foods.

"You're looking for the fancy book shop with the exclusive collection in the back room, right?" Luke asked.

"Yeah."

Luke shook his head and patted his friend on the back.

"You missed two turns. Come on. You'd never make it around here without me."

The shifter grinned and led his friend back the way they'd come past the crimson frontages of the high-fashion shops. It seemed that red and orange were the *in* colors that season. Luke glanced at the sparkly sweaters in the window and shook his head. He'd never be fashionable if it meant wearing things like that.

"What are you looking for in the book store anyway?"

Luke guided Tanner between the food stalls selling rich

and spicy meats which made his mouth water. They were going to eat with everyone else later. Maybe he could convince them to try that place.

"There's a book from Alison's childhood. She lost her copy years ago, but it helped her through some difficult times. It's called The Tales of Arashi."

Luke nudged his friend, "You're going soft, dude. You must really like her to be tracking down some obscure book."

"What's not to like? She's intelligent, strong, fierce, passionate, beautiful. I could go on for days."

Luke swallowed and changed the topic. His feelings for Izzie hadn't dwindled in her absence.

"I think we have a real chance at the Louper championship this year. The team's strong, and it'd be awesome to go out with a bang."

Tanner didn't miss the sudden switch in topics but let it slide.

"Hey, that's the store!"

The shop was nestled between a pair of jewelry shops sporting only the rarest and most expensive gems and metals. They didn't dare step foot in there. The book store displayed a range of leather-bound books with thick cream pages and handwritten texts in the left window. The right was saved for more modern textbooks and rare fiction books with short print runs.

They stepped into the warm store and looked around at the carefully arranged bookshelves trying to pinpoint the children's book section. Unlike more modern shops, there were no signs giving directions to the various areas. They wandered between the shelves full of tomes written in languages they didn't recognize and books on complicated sounding magic. Finally, they found the section they needed.

Tanner searched the shelf trying to pinpoint the book in question. Alison had mentioned it during her more vulnerable moments. It meant a lot to her, and he wanted a thoughtful gift to show her how much she meant to him.

Luke pulled the book off the shelf and winced at the price tag.

"Damn, she must be the one if you're paying that for a book."

Tanner gave a low whistle. He knew it wouldn't be cheap, but that was most of his savings. She was worth it.

They indulged in a large lunch in the food quarter. Tanner got a selection of the spiced meats he'd come across earlier, and Kathleen found some melt in the mouth cookies from a pair of bubbly wizards. Once they'd eaten, they split up once more. Christie went with Alison, Tanner, Emma, and Aya. They wanted to get Kathleen's gift without ruining the surprise for her. She went with Ethan and Peter to find Alison's gift.

"I saw the perfect earrings for Kathleen. They're made from a really rare gem, dwarven I think. They're stunning little roses, and the detail is just amazing. Each petal glistens and shines depending on its surroundings, so they'd go with any outfit she chooses," Christie explained.

"You think earrings are ok?" Luke asked the girls.

"Kathleen will love them. She likes sparkly things, and

like Christie said, they're unique. You can't go wrong with unique."

Something about Christie put Luke's shifter instincts on edge. He tried his best to relax and be nice to the girl, but he couldn't quite do it. She seemed nice, and she was certainly chatty, but there was something a little bit off about her. Maybe it was her Britishness.

"Have you made any progress on your missing books case?" Luke asked.

Alison sighed. She hadn't gotten anywhere at all, and it bothered her. She'd been into the library trying to find books on hiding your magic, but someone had already checked out any relevant texts. The gnomes refused to say who had done it. She had come to a dead end, and she hated it. Of course, she wasn't ready to give up yet. The thief would trip up; then she'd figure it all out.

"Oh, are people still worrying about those silly books? I'm sure it's all just a prank by one of the students. They'll show up in some hidden corner of the library or something," Christie said.

Luke looked at her warily.

"Look, here are the earrings! Aren't they just stunning? It says that each petal was handcrafted. Can you imagine how difficult that must have been? They're just so small, and each one is flawless. I can't imagine having steady enough hands to do that. I'm sure Kathleen will love them," Christie gushed, pointing at the earrings.

They crowded around the small display case and looked at the intricate piece of jewelry. The price tag was quite high, but it wasn't too much split between them. They wanted to get Kathleen something memorable. It was their last Christmas at the school together after all.

Tanner kept hold of the earrings. They had decided it was safer to keep them in the boys' dorm in case Kathleen got impatient and went looking for her gift.

"Are you excited about the Halloween celebrations, Christie?"

"I don't know much about them. Everything's very new."

Luke grinned. Halloween was always a lot of fun.

"It's when the veil between here and the World in Between thins. The magic becomes a little darker, and you can speak to the dead. Alison's magic will be really potent as she's a Drow," Aya said, waving to the rest of their friends.

Kathleen had a triumphant look on her face and carried a few small white bags. Peter was frowning at something in the palm of his hand, likely something to use in his science meets magic experiments.

"There will be a huge party. You're going to love it," Emma said.

Christie smiled and made a mental note of the upcoming event. Halloween was always spooky and fun in London, but it sounded like it'd be something else at the school. She was looking forward to a positive distraction.

CHAPTER SIXTEEN

Everyone crowded into multi-dimensional class the following day. Alison and her friends sat in the far corner close to each other.

"Everyone settle down. and let's get to work."

The students quieted and looked at Professor Wilson. Multi-dimensional was a class where they learned how to use their magic to get them out of sticky situations. It was something that had seemed even more vital since the fight before summer break.

"Today, you will be put into an earthquake situation. Earthquakes are a common phenomenon, and there is a real chance that you may well be struck by one. You'll take turns with the goggles and use your magic to remove yourself from the situation safely. Now, who's first?"

No one raised their hand.

"Rachel. Come along and show everyone how it's done."

The half elf tried not to roll her eyes as she stood up and went to the front of the class. No one wanted to go first, and the earthquake sounded like a hellish situation to be thrown into. She put the goggles on, and the classroom faded away, leaving her in a small basement type room. The tiled walls began to vibrate, and the plain concrete floor swayed beneath her feet. Slowly, the movement became more violent, and she looked for a way out. The narrow stairs began to crumble, and dust fell from the low ceiling. Panic constricted her throat.

She fought to calm herself and call up her magic. She needed to find a way out of this before she was crushed. Her magic came sluggishly in her panic while she looked around, trying to see how to use it. A small crack formed in the ceiling and dust rained from above, coating her and filling her lungs. She wiped her eyes and tried to stay steady on her feet as she looked at the newly formed crack. There was daylight up there. Maybe if she used some air magic, she could climb up through it.

A table fell onto its side, and the floor began to form dark hairline cracks. Rachel needed to move quickly; time was running out. Tiles fell from the walls and crashed onto the floor around her. The shaking and rumbling were deafening. She grabbed the table and dragged it beneath the increasingly large hole on the ceiling. Jumping onto the table, she pooled her magic around her feet and used it to push herself upwards. Scrabbling onto the edge of the crack, she pulled herself up into a plain white room. The roof had collapsed, but there was a clear escape route across the rubble out into the daylight and safety.

She formed a bubble around herself to protect her from the falling tiles and dust as she raced across the room and burst out onto the street panting for breath.

"That was a dangerous path, but you managed it. Well done," Professor Wilson said.

Rachel pulled the goggles off and took a long deep breath, glad to find the floor solid beneath her feet once more.

"Ben, you're up next." The professor pointed at a Light Elf who reluctantly stood.

When he put the goggles on, he found himself in an open street surrounded by palm trees. The ground split beneath his feet, leaving a great tear in the road. The bare earth walls of the hole were two stories deep, perhaps deeper. The ground bucked and shivered beneath him, and the buildings began trembling. He looked around trying to see somewhere safe to escape to. There was a small, open park on the other side of the chasm. The buildings were far enough away from it to make it the safest space he'd be able to find.

The palm trees buckled and cracked, falling near the fissure. Ben called his magic and focused on the tree nearest him. Its life force was still present. He wrapped his mind around the delicate threads and encouraged them to grow. The trees sprouted a sturdy trunk that stretched across the rift, giving him a bridge to run across. He released the life force once he was safely on the other side of the chasm and ran between the buildings. The earthquake's second tremor rolled through the city, and the buildings began to creak and crumble.

Ben called on his magic, feeling out the lifeforce of the trees and plants around the edge of the park. He pushed them to grow fast and dense, forming a secure barrier between him and the collapsing buildings. Glass shattered against strong trunks and boughs of the now tall mature trees. Bushes buttressed the fall of steel beams and lumps of concrete, leaving Ben safely in the middle of it all.

He pulled off the goggles, smiling and sweaty. "That was awesome!" He handed the glasses to a witch near the front.

Aya leaned over to Kathleen, watching as the witch slipped on the goggles. "I wonder if you can see people in one of these simulations. You know, relatives or friends."

"What are you doing? It isn't long until Halloween. Are you trying to speak to one of the dead?" Kathleen whispered.

"I'm not sure I want to mess with the World in Between," Aya said. "This is just a virtual lesson."

The World in Between was a place that contained the living and the dead, trapped together.

"Who do you want to see? Alison's a Drow. She has spooky magic that she has to explore on Halloween," Kathleen said.

Aya rolled her eyes.

"We've been there and done that. Remember what happened the last time? Doesn't seem like a good idea to play with that again. Some things are better left alone."

"Don't you want to talk to people who left? One last conversation?" Kathleen was pushing now.

She was still fascinated by the idea. Of course, it was easier for her because she didn't have anyone on the other side. It was always much easier pushing other people to do these things.

"No, I value the time I had with everyone, but I'm

sticking with the living. There's better things to do with our time, Kathleen."

Alison smiled before her attention snapped back to the witch at the front who was panting as she tried to climb a shaking building.

"Why is she going up? Surely she knows that's a stupid idea?" Kathleen whispered.

"People do stupid things when they're scared," Emma said.

"Do you have dates for the Halloween party? And dresses? I heard that Andrew was going to try and sneak some alcohol into the punch."

"He'll never make it past the gnomes or Miss Berens," Aya predicted.

"Kathleen, since you feel the need to chat, come and show everyone how this is supposed to be done."

Kathleen plastered a smile on her face and walked to the front of the class. She didn't know why they had to do these stupid simulations. She was never going to be stuck in a speeding car or an earthquake.

The classroom was replaced by a beautiful, white beach with resort hotels behind her and a string of palm trees along the edges. Kathleen listened to the eerie silence and watched as the water receded away from the beach. A tsunami was coming.

She had a few options that she had learned. She could either transfigure herself into a water creature and hope she survived the crush of the wave or form a bubble of air and sink into the earth to let it wash over her. As the huge wave began to approach, she steadied her nerves and called her magic. It flowed around her and quickly formed a thick bubble. If her math was right, she thought she had about five minutes of air.

The wave was almost upon her when she pushed her magic down into the earth, and her bubble sank into a deep dip. Her head and shoulders remained above the white sand, but the rest of her was buried in the earth. The wave crashed over her, turning her world into a wash of blues. Kathleen tried to keep her breathing calm and steady, so she didn't use up her air too quickly. The water raged around her, pressing against her magic and testing the boundaries she'd formed. She pushed more magic into it and tried to count down the time in her head. It must have only been a few seconds, but it felt like minutes had already passed.

The professor grudgingly allowed that. Kathleen handed the goggles back and walked victoriously back to her seat.

"Where were we? Oh, have you got your dress yet? I think I might go in something black with cobwebs. I might even get one of those silly pointed black hats. It's fun to play with the stereotypes, don't you think?"

"I think a few sophomores already had that idea. I saw one of them with a witch's hat this morning," Emma told her.

The Halloween party was an excuse to dress up and play with their magic. They enjoyed toying with the ideas and images that the humans had created about magicals over the centuries. It was quite common for the shifters to dress up as werewolves with furred faces and big yellow fangs. Not everyone found it funny though. Some found it very offensive. Kathleen just saw it as an excuse to be the center of attention. She would make sure that she had the very best outfit.

Alison was still thinking about approaching Tanner about speaking to his dead parents. She knew that she could help him do it, and it seemed like a nice thing to do.

Tanner had managed to secure a quiet seat at the front of the school under the drab grey skies. He'd been looking forward to a little alone time with Alison all morning.

"How were classes?" he asked, putting his arm around her shoulders as she sat.

"Not bad. I was thinking about Halloween though. We could talk to your parents, and you could say goodbye."

Tanner tensed and took his arm from around Alison's shoulders. He had no interest in doing such a ridiculous thing.

"No. I want to look forward, not back. We have a bright future ahead of us. I don't want to ruin that by digging up the past." He refused to look at her.

Alison reached out and put her hand on his cheek. She had expected him to be excited by the proposal.

"But surely you want to speak to them one last time? You must have unanswered questions?"

"I already said no."

"That's what Halloween is all about though. We have a chance to speak to the other side."

"Stop pushing this, Alison. I already said no. I don't know why you're so attached to this idea, but I said no."

"Why are you so against the idea?"

Alison stood, unsure what to do with herself. She had felt it was a good idea, something to help Tanner heal, and he wasn't even looking at her.

"I told you. I don't want to become lost in the past. Let me deal with my past my way. This is coming out of left field. I've never said I needed this. Just back off and drop it."

He also stood and shoved his hands into his pockets, looking out over the grounds toward the ragged pink edges of the horizon. Maybe he could go for a run to clear his head and get away from Alison's pushing. He didn't understand why she couldn't just drop the topic.

"Tanner, you're being ridiculous."

He turned to look at her. His eyes were stormy, and his soul flickered with anger. Alison had never seen him like that before.

"I'll see you tomorrow," he snapped then walked around her and went into the school.

They'd been planning on having some precious alone time later that evening. Alison sighed and let him be. He would come around once he'd calmed down. It was just the initial emotions clouding his judgement.

CHAPTER SEVENTEEN

Tanner was ready for the Louper game the following afternoon. He hadn't spoken to Alison since she kept pushing about talking to his parents. He pushed all of that out of his mind and focused on rooting for the Cardinals and the game ahead of them. They were up against the Kentucky Wildcats. Winning this would put the school one step closer to the championships. It was everyone's senior year, and he wasn't going to let them finish up as losers. They were going to go out with a bang.

Luke stretched and felt his wolf a little closer to the surface than usual. The Wildcats were a tough team to beat. His team gathered around him, tight smiles on their faces. They trusted him to lead them to victory.

"We play hard. We play to win. Remember, singularity of purpose."

Emma squeezed Alison's hand as Tanner sat down next to them in the stands. She knew her friend was worried about Tanner. He'd avoided her all morning. It wasn't like them to disagree, but it was a natural part of a relationship.

The fairies had claimed the top row of the seats and were chatting excitedly amongst themselves. Their wings almost glowed in the pale sunlight of the oncoming winter. The sky hung heavy and low with thick, pale grey clouds threatening an early snow. The Cardinals took their place on the field. A hush fell over the spectators as the game began.

The city of Prague popped up around the team. The team members stood still as the crowds of tourists bustled around them, and the harsh ringing bell of a tram cut over the unfamiliar language. A red tram careened around the corner, looking as though it should have fallen off its tracks. Its passengers stared unseeing from the windows; their expressions blank with a touch of contempt for their surroundings.

They stood in front of a white building with faux-stone arches over the windows and elegant balconies in front of the upper windows. It stood in stark contrast to the blocky communist style building next to it in a dark, dirty yellow with small square windows set back into the concrete. The dirty glass of the shop front almost hid the cheap clothing store within.

People muttered and pushed past the team as they tried to get their bearings and figure out where they should go from there. A woman in high heels huffed and hissed something rude under her breath as she barged past them and made a hand gesture in frustration.

"We need to start moving. What do those shifter instincts say?" Dan asked.

Luke turned a slow circle and felt a gentle tug toward what looked like it might have been a river.

"I've been practicing my tracking charms," Ethan said.

The team looked at him warily. Ethan meant well and worked hard, but his magic could be unpredictable, and they weren't sure if it was worth the risk.

"Go on and cast it while we move," Luke said.

He wanted to give his friend a chance. It wasn't Ethan's fault that he struggled, and a little confidence might help him find some more control. Ethan pulled out his wand and pushed his magic down the smooth piece of oak, using it to focus his magic. His thoughts wandered onto the image of victory, and a small puff of smoke emerged from the wand. He rolled his shoulders and brought his thoughts back to the tracking charm.

Slowly a pale blue orb bloomed from his wand, then it shot forward and floated down toward the river. The boys raced after it, weaving in and out of the groups of people who insisted on taking up obscene amounts of the sidewalk. Luke didn't understand how people could take up that much room without luggage or something else.

The buildings changed around them becoming more uniformly extravagant and expensive. They ran past a pale cream building with terra cotta colored panels painted around the windows and the intricate moulding. Another tram flew past them, ringing its bell. Ethan wondered why they were ringing the bell; then he saw a pair of pedestrians running across the road in front of the tram. They missed being run over by half a second.

The tracking orb started to rise when they passed a painfully modern building made of glass. It was shaped like a weird box. The boys paused in front of a theater. The lower level was formed of large, faux stone blocks with gaps big enough to use as hand and foot holds. Small faces watched them from the peak of the archways over the entryway to the building. Above the first floor stood a large open balcony area surrounded by Grecian style pillars that wouldn't be climbable.

Still, the orb moved upward toward the roof of the tall building above the intricate moldings depicting scenes of gods and angels. Luke put his hand over his eyes to shield them as he looked up and tried to follow the orb. There were statues up there of chariots with horses rearing up and women that he thought he recognized from a class in school.

The spectators gasped as the statues of Nike and Victory sitting atop the theater began to move. The horses' hooves stamped on the golden roof, and the goddesses with their wings stretched wide reached skyward. The wind fluttered their pale green garments as the tarnish from decades of cruel weather shook free. The horses neighed and shook their great heads in eagerness to be moving once more.

The goddesses shook their wings and snapped the reins on their respective chariots, pushing the horses forward off the roof. They charged out on thin air and began circling the theater. The Wildcats were the first to spot the gold disk shining in the sunlight on the back of Victory's chariot.

They looked up at the theater and the previously still statues circling it. If they timed it right, they could jump from the roof onto Victory's chariot. The climb up the theater wasn't an easy one once they reached the second story but since none of them could sprout wings, it seemed like the best plan.

Luke wasted no time in jumping onto the wall of the theater and began the grueling climb. He knew that Ethan and Rex had been working with their air magic. Between them, they'd be able to scale the building and retrieve the gold disk. The details eluded him at that exact moment as his arms started to ache where he pushed himself to climb faster. *Get onto the roof and go from there.*

Alison cheered for the Cardinals as the team began the difficult climb up the building. The Wildcats approached from the other side. They were climbing the shorter, simpler building which would make the leap onto the chariots more difficult, but it would take less time to reach the roof. Luke and his team were halfway up the main building topped with golden adornments when the Wildcats reached the roof of their building.

"Come on! Use your air magic and get us on that roof!"

Rex and Ethan both summoned their magic and tried to focus on the feeling of air pushing them upwards. It was difficult to weave the tricky magic while climbing the almost smooth building. They were trying to find holds between the artistic moldings. Feet slipped on angel wings and rested upon the faces of saints. They grasped onto whatever they could eager to reach the top.

The air magic slowly boosted them upward and gave them a small cushion when they lost their grip. The goddesses were circling at an even pace which made timing the jump onto the chariot somewhat easier. On top of the roof, the boys looked out over the city, a feeling of awe washed over them. Luke quickly pushed it aside and tracked Victory, slowly turning as he followed her, trying to find the best timing for the jump.

The Wildcats weren't wasting any time. Their most talented air mage took a running leap off the roof and used his magic to push him just far enough to grab onto the edge of Nike's chariot. The chariot dipped and wove. The horses screamed in fury, but the goddess remained uncaring as the young wizard hung, desperately trying to claw his way up. He finally managed to pull himself up and stood on a small section behind the goddess. There was a very brief window where she would fly near Victory. He just had to time it right, and the gold disk would be his.

"We will not be beaten," Luke growled.

"We have about thirty seconds before Victory comes back around. You can make that jump, and we'll back you up with some air magic," Rex said.

Luke rolled his shoulders and stepped onto the very edge of the roof. He had one chance, and there was no room for mistakes. He felt the soft tugging where his friends were forming the air magic to help him. Ethan gritted his teeth and focused. He wasn't going to be the reason Luke missed.

The Wildcats' wizard steadied himself as Victory started to come close. He saw the shifter on the Cardinals team preparing to make his leap. It was now or never. He launched himself into the sky, feeling absolute freedom for one blissful moment before he started to fall. His hand reached out, desperately clawing at the chariot's wheel. He clutched it with everything he had.

The chariot dipped when Luke landed with a soft thud. He snatched the gold disk, holding it up for everyone to see. The scene faded away, leaving the team exhausted and rightfully gleeful on the field where the spectators roared and cheered for them. Luke and Rex gave a small bow, playing it up for the crowds a little. They patted Ethan on the back.

"Well done. We couldn't have done it without you," Luke said.

"You too," he quickly said to Rex.

"It was all you man," Rex said.

The shifter was too humble to accept something like that. It was a team effort, and he had the best team he could ask for.

CHAPTER EIGHTEEN

The evening of the big Halloween dance had arrived, and the atmosphere throughout the school was electric. Alison and her friends were all sticking with the black and orange theme. Kathleen, not to be outdone by anyone, had found a stunning gothic gown. It appeared to be formed of layers of black spider's webs with glistening threads of orange woven throughout. She pinned a witch's hat barely as big as her fist on top of her elegant up-do and admired the entire thing in the mirror. With a swirl of her magic, her eyes brightened to bold emerald green and added some shimmering gold to her cheeks.

Alison had chosen something a little more subtle—a simple black dress slightly above the knee with a lacy square neckline and a pair of lacy flats. Aya and Emma were playing with a dark palette with heavy eyeliner and deep red lipstick. Their dresses were simple silk and satin affairs that flattered their figures without being too revealing. Christie had found a confection of ethereal black fabrics that floated around her and gave her a distinctly eerie appearance. She had used her magic to make her already pale skin even paler, and her golden hair took on a white sheen. Much to Kathleen's dismay, she was extremely eye-catching.

The guys arrived at their door in their blazers and black jeans. Tanner remained a little tense and hesitated before he put his arm around Alison's waist. She tried to ignore the tightness in her chest and focused on the happiness around her. The veils were thinner which meant the magic was a little darker, and she could feel it more closely. Everyone's souls were brighter and more vivid. She saw the sparks of excitement in her friends' energies and felt her concerns over Tanner slipping away. Everything would be fine once he'd actually spoken to his parents.

Halloween was a favorite event for the school. Everyone always tried to make the most of it. The halls had a thin mist crawling along the floors, and eerie dark forests replaced the usual walls. The dining hall itself had been transformed into a gothic castle with thick, heavy stone and low-hanging chandeliers. Whispers played just beneath the music, and everything felt that little bit spookier.

Shadows crawled along the walls as the students danced. Small black cats could be seen out the corner of people's eyes. As the night went on, pumpkins slowly appeared around the edge of the room and along the corridors leading to the hall. Over the course of a few songs, their grim expressions slowly became darker and more malevolent. Alison walked up to one and crouched to look at the magic within it.

To her delight, it was a complicated system of crystalline spells that interlocked and slowly evolved in time with the music. There was an internal clock that triggered something at ten pm. The humans thought that the witching hour was from three am to four am, but the kemana beneath the school gave it enough magic that the veil thinned at sunset and would remain thin until sunrise.

Alison turned to Tanner and took his hands in hers.

"We can speak to your parents. The veils are thin enough, and I know how to do it."

He didn't look at her for a long moment while he thought about it. She was so insistent, and he knew that she meant well. Maybe it wouldn't be such a bad thing to speak to them one last time. He had worked hard to look forward, but maybe that would help him heal.

"You're sure you can do it safely?"

Alison knew the veil wasn't something to play with. A lot of things could go wrong, but she was confident in her skills. Her magic had grown, and she'd grown along with it.

"Yes, and I'm sure we can find your parents."

They weren't the only students trying to speak with the dead that night. It was a time to say goodbye, and in some cases, try and gain what had been thought to be lost knowledge. Alison led Tanner away from the laughter and music filling the dining hall. She took him into an empty classroom, and he formed a series of small light orbs to allow them to see. The shadows receded to the depths of the corners, but still, a shiver ran down their spines.

The veil was right there. Alison felt as though she could touch it with her fingertips. Her magic came so easily as she focused on her task. The veil was so thin it looked almost entirely translucent when she managed to see it.

She reached out with her magic and gently tugged on a small section, intending only to form a small hole she could use to speak through.

The veil wrinkled and shivered but remained as it was. Alison frowned. She had read that this should be relatively easy. She pushed her magic against the veil and tried to make a small incision. Finally, it gave way, and the rush of cold magic washed over her, taking her breath away. She fought to hold the veil together while she called to Tanner's parents.

Tanner remained rigid next to her. This was seeming like a worse idea by the second. He should have told Alison no and left it at that. Then the familiar face of his mother appeared.

She was entirely white, but her warm smile was unmistakable. Tanner's stomach dropped, and his mouth went dry. He had no idea what to do or say.

"Tanner! Oh, I'm so glad I could see you again." The dead woman stepped forward with her arms outstretched.

Tanner didn't want to remember her like this. His memories were full of the beautiful living woman he had seen in pictures, not this white creature that made his stomach roil.

His father stepped forward and smiled kindly at him.

"We're sorry we left. We have wanted to see you one last time."

Tanner felt the progress he had made slowly unraveling. All the healing he had done since they had been taken from him. He had been doing well in school and looking forward to a bright future full of adventure. Seeing his parents again like this undid all of that. It was a stark reminder that they were gone and never to return.

"We miss you. I hope you're doing well," his mom said.

"Yeah. I'm… it's great. Everything's great."

Tanner wanted to leave and never look back. He wanted to remove the image of the spectres from his mind and cling to the happy memories.

"I'm so glad to hear that."

His mother looked behind her and smiled sadly.

"We're proud of you, Tanner. We always were. You're such a good boy."

His mother turned and walked into a small white light, having now said her final goodbye. Tanner clenched his fists and dug his fingernails into the palms of his hands. It wasn't supposed to be like this. He had already said goodbye at their funerals.

"You're going to go on and do amazing things, Tanner," his father said before he too slipped into the light.

Alison lost her grip on the magic, and something slipped between her fingers. A horse neighed in the corridor, and the unmistakable sound of hooves clattered down the hall. Alison ran out to look and saw a trio of what looked like huns galloping away from her down toward the dining hall. She squeezed her eyes closed and cursed.

A high-pitched giggle cut through the air. Suddenly, the tables and chairs flipped upside down and stuck to the ceiling above them. Alison saw a young set of twins, maybe six or so with little pig-tails, grin at her. They wiggled their fingers before they shot past her out of the door.

Tanner sighed and glared at Alison. Just when he thought the night couldn't get any worse, he realized he was going to have to corral the dead back to the World in Between.

Peter and Ethan looked warily at a tall man with short hair dressed in a black suit with sunglasses on. He had asked for a pen and paper from a pair of juniors.

"If you go ten paces to the east from here. Then dig beneath the tree with the big 'Y,' and you'll find it," the dead man said.

The juniors looked down at the roughly drawn map with frowns on their faces.

"This is supposed to be where again?"

"Well, if I gave you all the answers, then it wouldn't be any fun now would it?"

"Who did you say you were again?"

"D.B. Just call me D.B. I can't do anything with that there treasure, but you boys, you look like you're real adventurers."

"You are not traipsing through the American wilderness in search of non-existent treasure." Professor Grant sighed.

She looked at the hopeful faces of the students who were likely planning how to spend their new riches. It was all a joke to the dead man. If there had ever been any treasure, he had likely forgotten where it was long ago.

"Mr. Cooper, your treasure was found last week. I'm afraid that your business here has been concluded," Professor Grant said.

She had already had to fight with a particularly stubborn Roman centurion who refused to stop trying to get into the kitchens for the wine. He had finally relented, and she had managed to push him back to the World in Between. Still, there were many more dead around the school, and she was growing increasingly tired of their antics.

D.B. Cooper raised an eyebrow at the pretty witch and gave her a winning smile.

"Well, now that's a real shame. I must admit that I have other unfinished business though."

Professor Grant called her magic and gave him a small shove back into the World in Between.

"Remember, it's under the 'Y' tree!" he shouted, as he slipped back into the darkness.

"Did he give you a map too?" A couple of sophomore girls asked the juniors.

They compared their maps and found that it formed a more complete picture.

"That looks like the mountains near here, doesn't it? And isn't there a big Y shaped tree that got hit by lightning a century or two ago?"

Professor Grant took the maps from their hands.

"He was playing with you. Now, kindly go to your rooms."

The students eyed the maps rebelliously but let it slide.

Kathleen and Emma were facing down the Huns. The three warriors let out a battle cry as they urged their horses forward and pointed their swords at the two girls.

The witches weren't going to give in that easily. They pushed their magic into a heavy barrier at the last moment, and the Huns were thrown from their horses as they collided with the barrier. Alison summoned her Drow magic and pushed the fallen warriors back into the World in Between, ignoring their furious shouts and threats. She didn't speak Hun, but their tone made it quite clear they planned on doing her great harm.

The Huns had been far easier than the twins who were still running around the library frustrating the gnomes. They were trying to corral the little girls, but they moved the books around and caused havoc with the furniture floating and the bookshelves walking by themselves. The library was a catastrophe, and Leo Decker was at the end of his fuse. His poppy had stopped blowing raspberries and looked positively mutinous as the gnomes circled the little girls.

The girls gave the gnomes their biggest most innocent eyes, but they didn't believe it for a second. Alison saw the girls' magic forming in their hands behind their backs. She wrapped her own magic around them and dragged them back into the cold darkness of the World in Between.

"I'm not sure I want kids after those little hooligans," Emma said.

They took a moment to breathe. It had been exhausting running around the school trying to convince the spirits to return from where they came. A couple of the student's grandparents had been very insistent that they stay and tell their stories. Alison was glad she didn't see anyone she knew. Tanner hadn't looked at her since he had spoken to his parents, not that they'd had much chance to talk.

Something cold and wet dripped down the back of Emma's neck. A furious shout came from one of the gnomes. Emma cautiously reached back and felt the thick slime that was dripping from the ceiling onto her. It was going to take her an hour in a hot shower to get that off.

She looked around for the culprit. A quick shadow darted between the crooked bookshelves before a fresh pool of purple goo formed on the floor. Emma almost lost her balance but quickly righted herself. Alison was losing her patience and compassion for the spirits. She was sure it wasn't pleasant being stuck in the World in Between, but she was tired and wanted some peace, so she could speak with Tanner.

Emma leaned around the end of a bookshelf and saw an innocent little grandmother type with a long skirt and a long-knitted cardigan. The little, old lady formed a ball of magic and threw it at the back of Leo Decker's head. He spun around and glared at the dead woman with murder in his eyes.

Alison nodded to Emma, and they began a pincer movement around the woman who was focused on the gnome. Leo was dripping with a mix of lurid green and neon yellow goo. His shirt clung to his skin, and some of the foul-tasting stuff had gotten into his mouth. It was going to take an entire bottle of whiskey to clear that taste out.

Emma formed her magic and threw a net over the little old lady. Any innocence was dropped immediately as the woman turned to face Emma.

"I'm afraid your fun's over," Alison said, then she shoved her back into the World in Between.

"I think that's all of them," Emma said, trying to wipe the worst of the goo from her hair and neck.

"I hope so. I've lost all patience," Alison said, turning around looking for unusual magical signatures.

They checked every corner of the library and the corridors and didn't come across any more spirits. Emma went back to their room and hoped for a long hot shower while Alison looked for Tanner.

When they were alone again, Tanner turned to Alison with fury lashing through his energies.

"You did this, Alison. All because of your delicate ego. You should have left it alone. I told you I didn't want to talk to them, but you refused to leave it alone."

Alison was shocked at the harsh tone and words. She tried to reach out to Tanner, but he stepped away from her.

"No, you've done enough already."

"I wanted to help you. I was trying to-"

"To do what exactly? Show that you're the Drow princess, that you can dabble with the World in Between. We already knew that. I didn't need you screwing around in my past to know that. Do you have any idea how difficult it was seeing them like that? Do you even care?"

"Of course, I care," Alison whispered.

Tanner ignored her and stormed out of the room, leaving Alison feeling alone for the first time in years.

CHAPTER NINETEEN

Alison couldn't sleep, she was used to that, but her mind was too busy to meditate, so she got up as the sun rose. Her friends were buried beneath their blankets sleeping peacefully. The night before with Tanner and the dead kept playing on her mind. She had wanted to do something comforting and happy, but she'd managed to screw everything up.

The school was still messy from the havoc the dead had caused the night before. The cleaning staff was tidying away the remnants of broken chairs, loose papers, and scrubbing at unknown stains on the wooden floors. Alison felt bad for them. They didn't deserve such hard work, but there was nothing anyone could have done. At least, they had managed to corral the dead quickly and stopped them from wreaking mayhem on the town. The humans wouldn't have known what to do with that.

She stepped out into the fresh morning to see the frost glistening on the short grass. The pink sky was slowly turning back to a soft blue, and for a moment, everything felt ok again. There was something soothing about the familiarity of wandering around the grounds. It was a walking meditation. Her mind became calm, and she enjoyed the act of just walking and enjoying the cool air against her skin.

A quiet weight settled on her shoulders as she realized there were only so many more nights where she could walk through the short grass like this. The school had come to feel like a home, and her friends were her family. A glance back at the school brought a smile back to her face. She knew the bonds of friendship were too strong to be broken by distance. They had been through a lot together and had only grown closer because of it. It pained her to have lost most of her contact with Izzie, but she knew they would return to each other when things settled down.

The breeze picked up, whipping her long hair around her face. She pushed it away, and something fluttered near one of the trees, catching her eye. A square of white against the dark brown of the bush. When she approached, she saw it was a torn page from a book. The contents appeared to be from a transfiguration spell, and someone had crossed out a couple of the ingredients.

Why was the thief throwing away parts of the books? Alison looked at the page and wondered if perhaps she was being led into a trap. Or perhaps someone was being set up.

A clear, pale lilac trail formed when she looked at it with her Drow sight. The magic lit up like a beacon, and she followed it across the short grass toward the school. Trap or not, she wasn't going to ignore such a clear clue. If it came down to it, then she was comfortable with her battle magic and had proven she could look after herself. She pulled up some of her magic and kept it within easy reach.

The trail began a gentle curve back toward the school, and her excitement grew. It wasn't leading her in a worthless circle this time. She might finally make some real progress. The trail led through the front door and across the entryway. The clear lilac lines hovered just above the floor and stood in clear contrast to the dark wood and shadows of the early morning.

She followed it up the stairs that she had walked hundreds of times over the years she'd been in the school. An uncomfortable weight settled into the pit of her stomach. She knew this path too well. Maybe someone was screwing with her after all, or worse the thief was someone she knew.

The trail stopped dead at the entrance to the girls' dorms. She looked around trying to see if she'd missed something, or if perhaps it continued. Did she know the thief? Could it have been someone she spoke to every day?

It all felt a little too close to home. There was a chance the thief was involved in some very dark and dangerous magic. They could be right there near her own room and her friends. Once again, darkness lurked within reach, and she was determined to stop it.

On the way down to breakfast, Alison tried to catch Tanner's attention. His usual bright smile had been replaced with a heavy frown that made Alison's stomach drop.

"Hey, I found a clue with the stolen books this morning." She reached out to touch his arm.

He pulled away and put his hands in his pockets, his mouth thinned.

"Are you still trying to chase down that thief? Really, Alison, stop wasting your time."

His words stung. She knew she'd hurt him by pushing him to speak to his parents, but she hadn't expected the sharpness of his tone or the angry slashes through his soul.

"I'm not wasting my time. Someone is stealing books, and I think they're trying to do something dangerous. People could get hurt."

"I'm not interested." He turned to walk away.

She put her hand on his arm.

"Tanner…"

"No. Go and eat breakfast or study. I don't care. I'm not getting involved in your stupid book hunt."

With that he walked away, leaving Alison reeling. He'd been at her side. He'd helped her think outside the box and see things from fresh angles. And now, he was walking away leaving her feeling cold and alone.

CHAPTER TWENTY

The Halloween incident was all that everyone was talking about. A young wizard swore that he'd spoken to Elvis.

"He really is dead. I swear he told me he was planning on one last album, but then everything went black."

"Of course, you saw Elvis, Mark, and I'm the queen of Sheba," his elf friend said, rolling his eyes.

"Sure, so you'll believe that Huns galloped around the school and tried to capture Professor Powell's study, but you won't believe I saw Elvis."

"Yep. That about sums it up."

Tanner still wasn't talking to Alison, and the talk about the thinning veil and the dead only made that worse. Everywhere he turned he was reminded of that cursed night. All he heard was talk about who everyone had seen and how the Drow girl had helped send them all back again. Was it too much to ask for a little peace to get his head straight?

"The water turned cold before I could get that awful

goo out of my hair," Emma complained, as she braided her hair.

She was sure it still had a slight green tinge to it. She'd have to go to the kemana and find a special shampoo.

"The gnomes are livid. The library is a disaster. They've been trying to get the books back in their places all morning, but their spells won't work. Every time they think they have it straightened out, the books spring back off the shelves into untidy heaps everywhere," Aya said, looking out the window at the cold, dreary day.

"They think the twins put a minor curse on the place, and Professor Powell is investigating. Do you think he did anything special for Halloween? They say that he still has some dark magic within him, Halloween has to affect that, doesn't it?"

Alison raised an eyebrow at Kathleen's question.

"I'm sure he wouldn't have been hired if he was that dark."

"You're very defensive over him all of a sudden." Kathleen grinned, having found a fun new topic.

Alison had felt the way the veil affected her own magic and the power within her veins. She knew what she was and what that entailed but feeling it had been something else. She wasn't a malicious person, but there was a darkness and potential for harm within her. Professor Powell must have understood that feeling.

"Did you hear the stories Professor Hudson's great aunt told about her?" Aya asked, changing the topic before Kathleen pushed too far.

Kathleen was a good friend, but she needed direction and restraint, neither of which came naturally to her.

"No, tell us." Kathleen switched her attention to Aya, eager to hear some interesting gossip.

Professor Hudson wasn't Kathleen's favorite teacher, and she delighted at the idea of interesting stories about her existing.

Aya made herself comfortable on her bed taking her time to get the words straight in her mind.

"Her great aunt said that she was a real party girl when she was young. She would have a new boy on her arm every week, and she was a trouble-maker too. Apparently, she almost blew up her kitchen one morning when she was trying to create a forbidden potion. She couldn't afford the right ingredients, so she substituted the ground dwarven crystal and star flower for marigold and ground quartz. The explosion rocked the entire house and coated everything in thick, yellow dust that couldn't be budged!"

"There is no way that Professor Hudson was a party girl!" Kathleen exclaimed.

"She would sneak out on Fridays to go and dance with whoever her favorite boy was that week. Her aunt said that they tried grounding her, but she found ways around their spells. That was when they knew she had real talent."

"I think she was just telling stories to tell stories. Professor Hudson is far too straight-laced," Kathleen decided.

"I don't know. I think there's some hidden fun buried in there," Emma said.

"Alison, did you see anything in her energy?"

Alison gave Kathleen a pointed look.

"I can't see people's past via their energies. I can just see their mood and their magic."

"Some bounty hunter you'll be." Kathleen tossed a pillow at her.

Alison caught it and threw it right back. Pillows were soon flying around the room as the girls laughed and enjoyed the moment. After the stress and strain of Halloween night, frivolous fun was exactly what they needed.

Alison tried to talk to Tanner over lunch, but he refused to give more than monosyllabic answers.

"Have you tried talking to him about Louper? He has to talk to you about that," Emma offered.

"He still wasn't interested. He actually rolled his eyes at me," Alison said, watching Tanner's retreating back.

"What about buying him some of those little cakes he really loves?" Aya asked.

Alison pushed the last of her own lunch away, feeling frustrated. If only he would talk to her, they could work this out.

"No, that feels too much like bribery."

She didn't want to force him to be around her, but she missed him. It felt like a little piece of her was missing.

"I'll catch you guys later," she said, standing and heading out of the hall.

She couldn't fix her problems with Tanner, but she hadn't given up on finding the book thief just yet. It remained firmly in the back of her mind taunting her. Nothing new had come up. She had kept an eye out for more pages from books or weird magical trails, but nothing had shown up. The only oddity she'd noticed was the smudge in Christie's magic. It had become more persistent, and the girl had been evasive when asked about what was bothering her.

Alison had assumed that she was just ashamed at having to do extra practice with her magic, but now, she couldn't help wondering if perhaps there was something more to it. She knocked on Professor Powell's office door. As the dark magic professor, she hoped that he would know something about the potential transfiguration spell she suspected the thief was trying to commit. Maybe if she could figure out the spell, she'd be able to find the thief that way.

Professor Powell was lost in thought about the past. He had lived a long life full of adventure, but there were some things that he didn't share with anyone. Halloween night had brought back some of those memories and spectres from his past. He wasn't ashamed of his skills or the fact that he would do whatever it took to keep those around him safe. That didn't stop him from locking those memories away tight and the dark magic with it. His priorities and methods had changed, but he feared the time would come when he had no choice but to return to those ways. He thought back to Mara and sighed. They had been passionately in love at one time, and he would always care for her, but he didn't know if he could forgive her for hiding Izzie from him.

A knock at the door drew him from his thoughts. The students didn't often come to him because he wasn't as approachable as some of the other professors. He wasn't particularly surprised to find Alison Brownstone standing in front of him when he opened the door. The young Drow was a force to be reckoned with, and he suspected she was back to ask about the missing books. The determination shone in her eyes. The last he had heard she planned to follow in her father's footsteps, and he did not doubt that she would make a formidable bounty hunter.

"Come in, Alison," he said, gesturing to the seats in front of his desk.

He took his seat behind the desk and rested his hands on the wood. His space was neatly organized, everything had its place and could be found quickly and easily. There was an intensity to him that he was well aware of, it often made people nervous around him. Alison sat calm and confident as she looked into his dark eyes, and he resisted the urge to look away. He couldn't shake the feeling that she would be able to see every little detail of him should she so choose.

"I came here to ask you about transfiguration spells."

Xander smiled. He'd been correct. She was here to try and figure out the book thief situation. He leaned back in his chair.

"My speciality is dark magic, but I might be able to offer some advice."

"Well, I suspect that the spell in question involves dark magic. The books that have been stolen so far were all linked to transfiguration and the nature of a person's magic. I believe someone is trying to change their own or someone else's core magic type. That would fall under dark magic, wouldn't it?"

To alter the core of who and what someone was did fall under dark magic. It played with the very fabric of reality, and the risks were far too great. If Alison was right and someone was trying to change their magic type, then they were either very talented or very stupid. It would take a huge amount of skill and power to pull off such a thing and even then, there was a strong chance that they would die an agonizing death mid-change.

"Yes, that would be dark magic. I'm afraid I don't know any spells that do that specifically. I can, however, tell you that such a spell would require a lot of magic. I would expect the person to make use of one or more artifacts unless they're working with a group of other magicals. The type of change they're trying to bring about will obviously have an impact on what they need."

Alison thought back to the humans in the town and their artifact. Perhaps they would know something. She pushed that around her mind and remembered the fear and confusion on their faces when they had opened the box. No, they didn't know how artifacts worked. They might know where to source one from, but she'd have to sneak into town and ask around. That was a big risk. She considered it before she thanked Professor Powell and left.

She was one step closer to finding the thief she just knew it. They needed a dark artifact, so now she needed to find out where they could source such a thing.

Alison didn't return to her dorm room she had too much on her mind. Instead, she headed onto the grounds and slowly wandered through the woods and down to the stream. The flowing water helped her focus as she tried to organize her thoughts. If she wanted to go into town, she'd have to speak to Ethan, but she didn't know if it was a good idea to get him involved in this. No, she was still missing something. The magical trail had led to the girl's dorms, so maybe it would be better if she started there.

Dorvu was out chasing rabbits when she emerged from the woods. The large silver dragon flew close to the ground, puffing out streams of cold air, so the poor rabbits froze mid-step. The dragon scooped up his snack, looking very pleased with himself. Once his stomach was full, or he had run out of rabbits to terrorize, he began to fly higher. He amused himself doing acrobatics in the dark sky, diving down toward the ground, then pulling up before twisting and turning. Alison wondered if he was ok here at the school by himself. She hoped he wasn't too lonely.

She saw Horace's familiar bright red hair that almost seemed to glow under the lights around the barn. Her thoughts were reeling, and Horace had always been a steady and reasonable person to talk to. He offered her sound advice in a way that she appreciated.

"Good evening, Horace," she said, taking a seat on the bench next to him.

The familiar scents of hay and warm horses filled the air, and she felt some of her frustration easing. There was something soothing about the barn and talking with Horace. She reached down and scratched his dog behind the ear.

"And what's bothering you this evening?"

Alison wasn't sure where to start. She didn't like the situation with Tanner, and she needed to get a better grasp on the book thief. Although there was something more, something deeper, that was bothering her.

"Everything and nothing," she finally said with a short laugh.

"It's natural to be worrying about your future in your senior year. No one's going to judge you for that. Do you know what you're planning on doing?"

That was the heart of her problems. Horace had a real knack for getting to the crux of things and helping her work through her tangled thoughts.

"I'm going to become a bounty hunter like Brownstone."

"But you're worried because you're a Drow princess."

She frowned and ran her fingers through her increasingly white hair. It was there in the mirror every morning, the stark reminder of her heritage. There was no escaping it. Brownstone had fought the previous Drow queen to keep her safe. They would come for her again though. She was from the royal lineage and the next in line whether she liked it or not.

"Yes. It's an inescapable fact. I don't want those around me to be hurt because of my parents—my biological parents. And I don't know what impact that will have on me. Drows aren't really known for being the kind and loving types."

Alison had already felt some of her compassion slip away where her friends had remained kinder and gentler. She hoped it would be a benefit to her as a bounty hunter, but there needed to be limits. She couldn't allow herself to become as cold and cruel as the full-blooded Drow.

"You know I believe that there's good in nearly everyone. You have a good, kind heart, and you work hard to keep those you love safe. You're aware of what you are and your flaws, and you work hard to make sure they don't cause any harm."

Horace paused for a moment and considered how best to phrase this. The girl was struggling with her identity, but he saw good in her.

"You have a lot of magic in your blood, and a strong need to make this world a little bit better. Hold onto that, and you'll succeed. You'll make a fine bounty hunter, and your dad will be proud of you. The world needs a few more strong, good-hearted people like you, Alison. Don't you ever doubt that."

CHAPTER TWENTY-ONE

Alison stepped into the dining hall and wondered how it was Thanksgiving already. The months seemed to have flown by. The professors had really pulled the stops out with the decorations this year. The room was awash with fall colors. Kathleen hooked her arm around Alison's and led her to their usual table in the corner.

"Come on. I heard they're doing a feast for us."

Each table had been given a different style of decoration, and Alison struggled to take it all in. There was so much color and detail to see.

Their table had a beautiful deep orange tablecloth that shimmered with rich reds and golds. Their cutlery was neatly wrapped in a simple sackcloth ribbon with stunning leaves adorning it. Alison ran her fingertips over the leaves and found them to be soft silk. The colors blended beautifully, making them look real. The artist had even added in the small veins in a pale green and tan color.

The ceiling was covered in hanging fall leaves in every shape, size, and color. And an explosion of leaves erupted from the center reaching upward like a small tornado. The beautiful golds of magic thread formed a web around each leaf and held it in place. The magical overlay made it even more stunning to Alison's eyes.

As promised, they were given an absolute feast. Once Alison and her friends pulled their cutlery from their bows, the first course appeared on their crisp white plates. A generous matching white bowl of spicy squash soup in a rich umber color. The warm scent filled the air, combining with the sounds of laughter and feeling of happiness that permeated the room.

"This is amazing!" Emma declared as she took another spoonful of her soup.

Kathleen and Aya were a little more cautious, but Alison took a spoonful and found it to be perfect. It had just enough spice to be warming without overwhelming the mix of sweet and earthy. Everyone relaxed and talked freely, the weight of classes and the impending tests washing away.

"Did you hear about the junior who blew up the potions lab this morning?" Luke asked.

"Weren't they supposed to be making a healing potion?" Aya asked.

"That's what I heard," Luke said.

They all laughed. It must have taken quite a mistake to turn a healing potion into something explosive.

"The entire class was covered in green goop from what I heard. Professor Fowler still doesn't know what went wrong," Emma said.

Once the soup course was finished, a full turkey roast appeared in front of them, complete with sharp cranberry sauce, perfectly made mashed potatoes, and macaroni and cheese.

"I won't be moving for the rest of the day," Ethan declared.

"Worth it," Luke said as he finished his turkey.

"How's the car magic class, part two, going?" Ethan asked Kathleen.

She had managed to rearrange her schedule to include the advanced cars and magic class with the teacher she had a crush on. Kathleen gave a wicked smile. "I'm not sure. I think I might need some extra time with Professor Heineken."

Everyone laughed.

"Come on, he's not all that," Ethan scoffed. "You didn't crush on him like this last year."

"No, he's so much more and some things take time. I'm older now." Kathleen winked.

Dessert was apple pie and rich vanilla ice-cream with ginger beer to toast with. The pastry was crisp and flaky, and the apples were the right balance of sweet and tart. Alison was sure that was the best pie she'd ever tasted, and she wondered if she could get the recipe somewhere. It would be nice to try and make it for Shay and Brownstone at Christmas.

Kathleen lifted her glass. "This year, I am thankful for my friends. I couldn't ask for a better group of people. I'm also thankful for new opportunities, and the incredible fall line from Versace."

The warm glow of happiness suffused everyone, and Alison watched as gold hues spread throughout her friends and added small haloes of contentment. Even Tanner had a little ring of gold. He still refused to speak to her. She tried to forget about that and focused on the happiness. It was a time of thanks. Nothing else existed during that afternoon, and she hoped she could hold onto the memory and feeling for a long time to come.

Emma chewed her lip a moment before she lifted her glass. "I am thankful for a good education, incredible food, and good health. I hope I don't need to remind you that I'm thankful for all of you." She grinned.

"You're such a dork," Kathleen teased.

"I'm thankful for a good pack, a fantastic Louper team, and my family and friends," Luke said.

Aya squeezed his lower arm and smiled at him.

"This year, I'm thankful for the teachers and friends who have given me the confidence and belief in myself. I'm thankful for my family for always being supportive, and that this school exists. It gives me a sanctuary and a place where I can practice my magic amongst my best friends," Aya said.

Emma reached over and hugged Aya. "I'm so proud of you."

Aya flushed a little and smiled broadly.

Ethan took a deep breath and held his glass high, "I'm thankful for having this opportunity to live a better life. I'm thankful for all that I've learned about my magic and for my health. There were times when I thought I'd be stuck on the streets, but I'm here, and for that, I will be forever thankful." He couldn't hide the slight wobble in his voice.

"I'm thankful to be here with all of you," said Tanner.

The girls got up and pulled him into a big group hug that almost suffocated him before it was Alison's turn.

"I am thankful for these glasses that allow me to see the world in a whole new way. I'm thankful for every one of you and for all help you've given me. I'm thankful for my adopted parents, and the support they've given me over the years. And I'm thankful for that incredible apple pie!"

Everyone clinked their glasses and drank deeply allowing the comfortable silence to wash over them before Emma asked, "Do you think they'd let us have more of that apple pie?"

"I don't think I can eat another bite," Luke admitted.

"I bet you would if more of that pie appeared on your plate," Kathleen teased, nudging him.

"I can't say for sure that I would be able to resist."

They all laughed and relaxed in their chairs, unwilling to leave just yet.

Mara looked around the hall at the laughing and happy students and felt a swell of pride. The decorations were perfect. A cornucopia sat in the middle of the professor's table, woven from pale yellow reeds and full of small pumpkins, berries in shades of reds, yellows, and oranges, and large fall leaves. Ribbons hung around the edges of the hall, each decorated with glittery acorns and berries. The ceiling had been quite a challenge to get it just so. The leaves were suspended with thin threads of golden magic holding them in place.

Candles in the traditional fall scents were carefully

scattered throughout the room, filling the air with scents of falling leaves, crisp frosty mornings, and cinnamon. She closed her eyes for a moment and breathed it all in, allowing it to fill her with the sense of comfort and happiness that came with these things.

Xander remained quiet and withdrawn, but he had a smile on his face for the first time since she'd had the discussion about Izzie with him. Thanksgiving meant putting aside such concerns and focusing on the positive things around them.

She lifted her glass of traditional elf wine. "I am thankful for the talented faculty, supportive friends, generous and skilled students, and the opportunity to shape the next generation into something positive."

Her fellow faculty members lifted their glasses and all said, "Let us give thanks."

Xander squeezed her hand when he thought no one else was looking. A small, warm smile formed on her face as she appreciated the gesture. They would never be what they once were, but she had found that the little things often counted the most.

"I am thankful for magical soap, and students that keep me on my toes," Lucy Fowler said.

They laughed and raised their glasses to her. News of the explosion in her lab had passed through the school like wild-fire. They still hadn't managed to find out how the student did it. Thankfully, it wasn't anything harmful, although a couple of the desks would forever be marred with green splodges, they were functional enough.

Christie had never celebrated Thanksgiving before. She knew that it was a big holiday for Americans, but she never dreamed it would be quite this overwhelming. The hall had been transformed into an autumnal wonderland. Everywhere she looked, there were stunning splashes of golds, oranges, and reds. Leaves hung from the ceiling as though she were sitting beneath a grand oak back in London. The air was thick with the smell of warm apple pie, cinnamon, and fresh frosty mornings.

Each table had been decorated differently. She made her way between them, admiring the complicated arrangements of glittery acorns around beautiful pumpkin shaped candles. Another table had an intricate wreath edged with wheat, berries, and leaves. In the center was a simple ceramic bottle painted in a gradient of oranges that said, 'give thanks' in an elegant white script.

She tried not to stop and look too closely, but there was just so much to take in. Her new friends had claimed the table near the western edge of the room, and she was delighted to find a seat left open for her. Their table had a centerpiece formed of a wrought iron base with twisted arms that gently curved upward and were topped with dark red and orange glittery candles at each end. In the very center was a careful arrangement of what looked like a mix of ceramic and silk leaves, pumpkins, and berries. She reached out and found it to be slightly warm to the touch.

"This is incredible. I've never seen anything like it," she said.

Rachael grinned at her and put her arm around Christie's shoulders.

"We don't do things small or by halves around here."

"I can see that! We don't have Thanksgiving in England. I've heard of it, but we don't actually celebrate it. It seems like a really nice holiday. This is all so wonderful."

The words tumbled out of Christie's mouth. For the first time in a long time, she was surrounded by friends. The school had been scary and difficult at first, but that day, she could be entirely herself without fear or worry about what people would think.

"To new friends, awesome food, and a break from classes," Sarah said, lifting her glass.

They all followed suit, "to new friends!"

Christie looked down at her drink when she tasted the warm burn of ginger on her tongue. She hadn't tried ginger ale before. It was available in London, but she'd never really felt the need to try it.

"Don't you like it?" Sarah asked.

"You've never had ginger ale before!?" Bea said in mock horror.

"No. I've had cream soda. I love that, but I've never had ginger ale. It's not available everywhere in London, and well, it sounded a bit weird."

The girls around her grinned and held their hands out. Christie took Sarah and Rachel's hands and followed along as they all gave thanks.

When it came to her turn, she said, "I'm thankful for my parents, my friends, and everything that's to come this year."

Everything was going so much better than she'd dared hope, and she knew that no matter what came happened this winter she'd be able to overcome it.

CHAPTER TWENTY-TWO

Alison managed to find a quiet corner in the library to talk to Tanner. The rain trickled down the windows and added darkness to the usually bright space.

"You should have respected my wishes," Tanner said quietly, looking out the window.

He had been quiet and lost in his own mind for a few days. He'd tried to focus on classes, but the images of his parents haunted him. His mouth went dry at the memories.

"I'm sorry. I... I didn't really think about your perspective."

Tanner looked at Alison. She watched as the thick strokes of anger slowly subsided into something less aggressive. He still kept his legs bent forming a barrier between them. She missed him, the gentle contact and feeling that she could be vulnerable with him should she need it.

"We're almost halfway through our senior year..."

Alison had been thinking about the future a lot. Time

was ticking by, and she needed to decide how she was going to achieve her goals.

"I'm thinking about taking a gap year and becoming a bounty hunter like Brownstone. I'm pretty sure that's what I want to do with my life but taking that year would let me be certain. Not sure how Dad will take it, we'll see."

Tanner shook his head. He had thought there was a small chance for them to get back on track, but she had thrown a wrench in the works. Of course, he supported her dreams, but she knew that he couldn't go with her on that. If nothing else, Brownstone didn't approve of him.

"You know I can't join you on that."

Alison felt a weight form in the pit of her stomach. There was no way around the fact that her choosing that path would keep them apart for the year. They might be able to meet up here and there, but it wouldn't be the same. That was her dream though. She wanted to follow in Brownstone's footsteps and make a difference in the world.

"I'll see you later," Tanner finally said.

He couldn't shake the feeling that maybe this was it for them. Alison had her dreams to pursue, and they didn't involve him. He wasn't sure what he was going to do with his own future right then. College seemed like a good idea, but he hadn't settled on a real plan. He wasn't going to stand in her way, that wasn't fair to her. She had worked far too hard to give everything up for him.

Alison tucked her legs underneath her, and Kathleen put her arm around her shoulders, pulling her friend close.

"I'm sure it's not that bad. You're both passionate people, and it's only a little break. You'll be back to something from one of those romance movies in no time."

"Everyone sees the way Tanner looks at you, and you can see the affection and care in his soul right?" Aya asked as she sat down on the bed with Alison.

They were used to seeing the Drow fierce and strong, and this small shred of vulnerability worried the girls. They crowded around her and lit candles to give the room some warmth and comfort.

"Really, I wouldn't worry at all. He'll see sense and remember just how important you are to each other. I'm sure you're made for each other." Kathleen squeezed her friend's shoulders to emphasise her words.

"He was so angry. I think I really screwed up," Alison said quietly.

"We all screw up. It's natural and part of life. What matters is that you understand that, and you're trying to do what's best for Tanner. You're giving him a little room, and you'll soon bounce back," Emma reasoned.

Alison nodded to herself, of course, her friends were right. It was just a little glitch. She wasn't going to sit around and mope. It was likely nowhere near as big as it felt. And if it was, then she had a bright future ahead of her. As much as she cared about Tanner, she wasn't going to allow herself to wallow in possibilities and maybes.

The girls all squeezed onto the bed and hugged Alison tight, relieved to see her returning to herself quickly. She was the strongest of the group, and they didn't know how to react to seeing her like that.

Alison enjoyed the support and comfort of her friends.

She felt her assurance and confidence coming back as she realized it was just a small argument. She had her friends around her. No matter what happened, she'd never be alone in the world. She would handle whatever life threw at her with strength and dignity.

The rehearsal for the musical gave Alison exactly the type of distraction she needed. She'd learned her lines and felt good about her harmonies, but she was struggling a little with the dance routines.

Christie was distracted throughout the rehearsal, and Alison noted the darker grey smudge in her magic. She sang her songs beautifully but remained away from the main group of students who had formed a tight-knit bond over the rehearsals.

The younger girl slipped out of rehearsals early and didn't say where she was going. Alison was growing worried about her, but she couldn't help feeling a little suspicious. The magical trail had led to the girls' dorms after all.

"Alison, stop daydreaming. We need to go through this song again. From the top."

She gave Professor Fowler a polite smile and tried to remember which song they were rehearsing.

The opening bars of music for *I'm Not That Girl* began to play, and Alison found herself thrown. It struck a little too close to home at the moment. The song was Elphaba convincing the audience that her flaws were too great, and she would never earn the love of the man she'd fallen head over heels for.

Her emotions shone through as she began to sing. Her place in the world was a difficult one, and she was aware of her flaws, but as she sang, she started to convince herself that she deserved far more. Horace had been right, as he usually was. She was a Drow. Yes, she had the potential for great cruelty in her blood, but there was a positive side to that. She had a strength of mind, magic, and body that allowed her to protect and help those weaker than herself. She put her heart into the song and became more certain that being a bounty hunter was the perfect path for her.

The words stood in stark contrast to her own feelings as the final verse came around. She sang about not daring to wish for something she would never have. It was a difficult and heart-breaking song when sung well, but she used it to empower herself.

Everyone cheered and clapped when she finished, and she took a small bow. Flynn who was playing the love interest of Elphaba who was convincing the audience she didn't have a chance with came over and congratulated her.

"You have a beautiful voice. I'm really glad Professor Fowler picked you as Elphaba. Can you believe we'll be fitted for our costumes soon? It seems like it's come around too fast."

Time had slipped through Alison's fingers as she realized just how much time had passed since her audition. Flynn was a Light Elf who had started the rehearsals quiet and reserved, but he was coming into his own.

"I'm sure we'll be ready for our big performance next

semester. The costume department seems to be really excited about the costumes, and the scenery is coming along nicely."

"Beautiful! Now, where is my Glinda?"

Kathleen squeezed Alison's hand as she walked past her and took center stage. She was made to play the good witch. Alison may have been born with darker blood, but she would show the world that she was far more than her heritage.

Alison desperately wanted to go and find Christie, but Professor Fowler insisted that they all stay while the ensemble went through their parts. She knew that she should be more focused on the musical given it was important to her, but she was worried that her friend could be in trouble. Or she could be trouble that would bring harm to her friends and potentially the school. Whatever Christie's role, Alison needed to find out and put a stop to it.

Alison went looking for Christie once the rehearsal concluded. She looked in the windows of the classrooms as she passed and saw Aya in her art group. The students were sitting in front of small lumps of clay that they molded using their magic. Aya was focusing with a deep crease between her brow as her clay slowly formed a delicate daisy. Alison was impressed and made a mental note to ask Aya about it. She hadn't mentioned being such a talented artist.

Another classroom was occupied by the debate club who were furiously debating whether or not to trust the human government. That was a particularly hot topic amongst magicals. Most people didn't think they could trust the human government at all, but others wanted to see some good in them. Alison herself wasn't entirely sure. She didn't really have a head for debate and preferred to use her magic and fists to resolve problems. There weren't going to be many opportunities to debate a dark witch or wizard into stopping whatever illegal activity they were partaking in.

The hallways were mostly empty as students were either studying or in after class groups. Alison was ready to give up on finding Christie when she spotted a familiar blonde head. Something stopped her from calling out, an instinct that told her to remain quiet and see what Christie was doing.

Alison stepped into an empty classroom where Christie was moving her hands in a rhythmic pattern required to weave a spell. The dark smudge in her magic had grown into something darker, and there was a heather grey wisp of magic forming between her hands. Alison didn't recognize the exact spell, but she knew that it wasn't something a student should be doing. She had hoped that Christie was just practicing for one of her classes, but none of the professors taught anything like that. Christie hurriedly stopped and gathered her things as Alison walked into the room. She shot out of the other door and vanished down the hallway before Alison could say anything to her.

Christie was out of sight by the time Alison went back into the hallway. She tried to see a trail of magic and came up with nothing. Alison jogged down the hallway thinking that she could catch up with the other girl. There were only so many places to hide and turn after all. After ten minutes, she had to admit defeat. The girl was nowhere to be found, and she had no clue where she might have gone.

Alison realized that Christie had never told her which dorm room hers was. When she thought about it, that was quite an oddity. The younger girl had always come over to Alison and her friends' room. The idea that she was hiding something was growing by the minute. There was certainly something wrong with Christie. She hoped that she was blowing things out of proportion, and there was an innocent explanation for everything, but Alison was beginning to suspect that Christie wasn't as naive and delicate as she initially appeared.

It wouldn't be the first time a dark magic student had been planted in the school. Tanner had been a toombie as they called them originally. He had never quite gotten over that fact as he had no idea it had happened. Alison frowned and hoped that Christie was equally as unaware of the situation.

CHAPTER TWENTY-THREE

Alison hadn't seen any sign of Christie since she vanished out of the classroom. She had asked Emma and Aya if they knew where her room was, but neither of them did. Her suspicions were growing, and she wasn't sure how much to involve her friends. She didn't want to put them at risk but knew they might be able to help.

"I think she might be involved in the missing books," Alison whispered.

Aya frowned. "She's only a freshman. How could she get around the gnomes' magic?"

Alison hadn't figured that part out yet. Christie hadn't shown any exceptional talent for magic that she'd seen. The girl's magical aura was typical with a slight leaning toward plants and potions. There was that grey smudge though, some darkness within her that could be affecting her. Maybe that was a mark of the dark artifact tied to the transfiguration spell.

They arrived in Professor Powell's dark magic class and settled down in their usual seats. No one could focus with the end of term being so close, and the last thing on anyone's mind was studying. They were all far too excited about heading home for the holidays and getting some time away from class work.

Xander looked around the room at the students and felt his jaw tighten. They were all gossiping and fidgeting. Not one of them made any attempt to look at the front of the class. These students were the next generation, those they were training to keep the world safe.

Safe from the likes of me, he thought for a moment. The dark magic would always be a part of him. It called to him during the long cold nights and tempted him during moments of weakness. These students needed to understand what was out in the world.

He understood that they were coming to the end of the year, and everyone was tired from the incident at Halloween, but that didn't excuse a lack of discipline. If they showed a lack of focus during an attack, they could get themselves killed. He squeezed his eyes shut for a moment and tried to quash his frustration. The students weren't the problem. He was still thinking about Mara and the fact she had hidden Izzie and the truth of who she was from him. He could have kept the girl safe. He had more than enough magic at his fingertips to remove whatever threat might occur.

Another look around the classroom at the gossiping students hardened his resolve. He was going to push them and make them really work. The days were ticking by, and they needed to be ready for whatever the world threw at them.

"That is quite enough. We will start today's class with a sanity attack. Aya, prepare yourself."

Aya had no time to understand what was happening before Xander had made a small motion with his hands forming the dark magic and threw it at the girl. She tried to pull up her magic to protect her mind, but she was too slow. The words wouldn't form on her tongue, and the spell sank into her mind.

The classroom was quickly replaced with a small, dark room that smelled of dampness. Something was in there with her. Something dangerous and hungry. Her heart rate quickened, and her mouth went dry. Fear threatened to consume her, but then the scene changed again.

The room shifted, and suddenly she was balancing on the edge of the cliff. The waves crashed against the stone beneath her. She was terrified of heights, and her panic almost claimed her entirely. The students watched in horror as Aya sat frozen, her skin pale and clammy, and her mouth gaped open in a silent scream. Whatever spell Professor Powell had cast left the girl terrified and unable to move.

They had only seen a spell like that once before, last year. It sent a chill through the room.

Professor Powell had been teaching them defense against attacks, ranging from fire and shadow through to vicious spells that ate at bones and would stop a heart dead if you weren't quick enough. This was something new for them to learn. It seemed to be attacking Aya's mind, and that shook some of the students.

Alison wanted to help her friend, to free her from her torment, but she understood that they needed to be able to look after themselves. Aya found some semblance of calm and pulled on her magic with everything she had. She waved her magic in front of her face and barely whispered the sloppy mental fortitude spell, but it was enough to give her some breathing room.

The cliff sank away, and the scene turned into a dark, desolate land. Coyotes yipped somewhere around her, and something large bayed for her blood. She knew that this was just the spell, and the words came to her more clearly this time. She ground them out and pushed as much of her magic as she was able into it. The mental fortitude spell worked, and the dark magic snapped, leaving Aya panting and slumped in her chair.

Professor Powell was disappointed that it had taken Aya as long as it did to break his spell. If she had been out in the world, she could have been killed. She was too vulnerable while she was locked in her own mind panicking. He made a mental note to add more mental defenses to his list of spells to teach.

"Not bad. Ben, you're next."

"He's in a foul mood," Kathleen hissed.

Emma reached over and tried to soothe Aya as she calmed herself and dug her fingertips into the wood of her desk. It was just a test. It wasn't real. She grounded herself with the physical sensation of the wood beneath her fingertips and tried to shake off the vile dark magic.

"I heard he had some argument with the headmistress, and he hasn't let it go yet," their classmate Stephanie murmured.

Professor Powell heard her and threw a dark spell at Stephanie. She put up a hasty mental protection spell and fought with the dark magic. It was a writhing mass of pure darkness to Alison's eyes.

"I don't think I've ever seen him this bad," Emma whispered.

"He'll hurt someone if he's not careful," Kathleen muttered.

Stephanie's hands shook as she tried to form the right gestures and words to protect her mind. The mass of dark tentacles was slowly sinking into her aura and wrapping around her head in Alison's vision. A shiver ran down the girl's spine. Fighting to protect your body was one thing, but the mind was something else entirely.

The spell snapped and vanished when Stephanie shouted the final word of her spell and glared at Professor Powell. The professor's expression remained one of mild frustration. She had done better than Aya, but it was still sloppy, and he didn't appreciate her attitude.

"Split into three groups," Xander commanded.

He wasn't in the right frame of mind to be dealing with the students. He decided he would set up some tests and let them work it out for themselves.

The students split into three roughly equal groups, and Xander sent a small swarm of blood-thirsty sprites at one group. He formed a shadow spell that acted much like quicksand and slowly pulled the middle group down into the floor. The final group received a slavering hell beast. He formed small barriers, so each group was truly separated, and the creatures couldn't leave the classroom.

He had been trying to find Izzie and her parents so that he could offer them some aid, but they were truly hidden. That wasn't such a bad thing. If he couldn't find them, neither could their enemies. It still didn't sit well with him. He raked his fingers through his greying hair, frustrated. He had lost too many years.

Kathleen, Alison, and Emma were in the group with the vicious sprites. The small creatures were barely six inches tall, but their tiny dark frames were packed with pure malice and ill-intent. Their mouths were full of sharp razor-like teeth, and their hands and feet were tipped with equally sharp claws. Even their translucent fluttering wings were sharp. Everything about them was designed to tear into larger beings and bring them down.

The sprites huddled near the ceiling above the students, plotting their demise. The students looked on in dismay.

"What if we fry them?"

"They're fire resistant if I remember correctly."

"What about forming an energy shield and crushing them?"

"Ew, that'll be a horrible mess and an awful way to die. Imagine if someone slowly squeezed you to death."

"Well, what's your bright idea, genius?"

"The professor didn't say we had to kill them. He just said we had to deal with them." Emma ducked as a sprite flew at her face. "So why don't we form a box and lock them in it?"

"No, you must return them to where I summoned them from," Professor Powell informed them.

Peter flattened himself under one of the desks when the sprites started forming an organized swarm and looked right at him.

Ethan looked into the beady eyes of what he thought was the lead sprite and focused on his magic. His wand grew warm in his hand. He was going to send that vicious little monster back where it had come from. Of course, the fact he didn't know where it had come from meant this idea was doomed from the start. His banishment spell flew from his wand and hit the sprite squarely in the middle of its chest. It screamed, and Ethan's eyes went wide as the other sprites bellowed a chilling war cry and aimed right for his face.

He tried to run between the desks with the pack of furious sprites right behind him, but the desks kept slowing him down. The other students threw banishment and explosion spells at the sprites which only antagonised them further. They split into what could only be described as hunting parties and began systematically attacking everyone who had dared throw any magic at them.

Alison swatted one away and received a deep cut to her hand for her trouble. She knew the banishment spells weren't working, but she hadn't figured out which spell they needed yet. Her Drow magic pooled within her and promised she would end the sprites swiftly, but that wasn't the solution here. The sprites were hardy little beasts with thick magic-resistant hides and had far more intelligence than should be able to fit into such a tiny skull.

Kathleen was growing increasingly angry as the sprites tangled in her hair and tried to claw at her face. She wrapped her fingers around one and threw it at a desk. It bounced once and returned to trying to cut her eyes out. The cuts on the students were growing deeper, and their tempers were fraying. Professor Powell remained behind his desk going over papers.

Peter cast a shield spell over the sprites hoping to

contain them. It limited their movements for a few precious moments. It gave Kathleen enough time to clear her head and form the words in her mind. She had learned a particularly potent explosive spell. Those sprites were going to be nothing more than specks of red dust when she was finished with them.

The room hummed around Kathleen as she pulled up the necessary magic. She threw the spell at the sprites only to see the large ball of fire growing far bigger than she had intended. It was supposed to be the size of a basketball, and yet it was growing by the second. It would consume the entire classroom along with the sprites.

Professor Powell saw what was happening and jumped up, but not before Alison threw a protective bubble of energy around it that enveloped the sprites and the fire. The stench of cooked sprite filled their nostrils and made a couple of the students gag, but it was better than being cooked themselves. The fire crackled and went out, leaving nothing behind but grey ash.

"Well done, Alison," Xander said with a small nod.

The young Drow had real potential, and Xander hoped that she continued to learn and grow. She could make a difference in the world.

The first group of students slouched in their seats as they watched the other two groups battle with the shadow and the hell beast. The shadow was slowly sucking a young, green-haired witch into the floor while they grew increasingly concerned.

"Think! What would defeat shadow?" Professor Powell asked.

"Light! We need light!"

"We tried light already!"

"We need to focus it and cut through the shadow."

Two of the students were up to their waists in the shadow now, and they were eager to do whatever they could to get out of it. They worked as a group and spoke the words together. A blinding explosion of light removed the shadow and left the students sprawled out on the floor.

"I think we got the best deal with the sprites," Emma said.

"They're not covered in cuts," Kathleen complained.

She caught the look on Alison's face. "Thank you for your help. I couldn't have done it without you."

CHAPTER TWENTY-FOUR

T he nurse had patched everyone up with an efficiency that came from years of practice. Alison left everyone to get their injuries seen to and looked for Tanner. She hated arguing with him and wanted to clear the air.

"Can we talk?" She touched his arm to get his attention.

The furious red lines weren't in his soul this time, and she appreciated that.

"Ok." He walked toward the bench where they often spoke.

It wasn't quite the enthusiastic response that Alison had hoped for, but it was better than nothing. She knew what she wanted to say, and she had decided that if he still didn't want to speak to her afterwards, then she would accept it. Tanner was an amazing guy, but she wasn't going to allow their differences to ruin her year.

They stepped outside into the cold, damp day and sat down on the bench. Alison held her coat close to her and wished she'd grabbed her scarf and gloves. It was far more bitter out than she had expected. Tanner looked at her expectantly.

"I'm sorry. I should have respected your boundaries. When you said no, I should have left it at that." She looked away. "I really wanted to help you heal, but I know everyone does that in different ways."

Tanner smiled. He didn't need Alison's ability to see souls to know she was sincere in her words.

"I know you didn't mean any harm. Next time when I say no, just listen." He sighed. "Seeing my parents really threw me. I had accepted a long time ago that they were gone, and I got on with my life. Then they were right there, and all of those old, ancient wounds reopened."

Alison reached out to take his hand. She didn't know what to say.

"The years without them haven't been very easy. I have good friends around me, and that helped a lot. I'll never forget them, but I don't want to think of them as those ghostly shadows of real people."

Alison knew it must have been hard on him. She thought about her mother sometimes, but she didn't have the emotional wounds that Tanner did.

Tanner squeezed her hand and gave her a soft smile.

"I missed you. I was angry at what you'd done, at your lack of respect and caring about my wishes." He took his hand away again. "It was easy being mad at you, but it was a shallow anger to try and hide the pain. I didn't like being away from you. Nothing compared to seeing your smile in the mornings or feeling you close to me when we sit and enjoy a peaceful silence."

"I hated being away from you. I care about you, and you give me a strength that nothing else can bring. You're always so insightful, and you offer views and opinions that I need to hear. I missed your presence and all the comfort that brings."

Tanner put his arm around her shoulders and gently pulled her closer.

"Tell me about these missing books then."

Alison smiled, leaning into him.

"I found a page from a missing book out near the woods. I'm pretty sure it's part of the spell to do transfiguration, which fits into our theory about someone trying to change their magic type. I followed the trail back to the girls' dorms."

Alison let her words and their implications sink in.

"So, you think it's a student here at the school? And they're trying to transform their magic type?"

"Yes. I'm…" She tried to think how to put it. "I'm concerned that it might be Christie. It's weird that we don't know what room she's in, and she's had a dark grey smudge in her magic for months now. Emma and Aya said they've heard an odd clicking sound when they're around her. I also saw her performing a spell in an empty classroom. She ran when she saw me, and I haven't been able to ask her about it."

"Well, that is pretty damning. Have you told anyone else?"

"No, I wanted to run it by you first. In case I'm wrong, I don't want to tell Professor Powell. It could harm her reputation or even get her kicked out of the school."

"What other reasons could there be for the smudge and the clicking?"

"Well, the smudge is from some form of unpleasant magic. I'd thought it was a remnant from a class at first, and she is clearly practicing magic between classes. I suppose she could be trying to practice her defense against dark magic. Professor Powell has made no mention of that, and he isn't really the type to give tutoring outside of classes. She could be under the influence of a hex or other dark spell and not be aware of it."

"And if she's under someone else's influence then we need to find out who, how, and what consequences there are."

Alison smiled up at Tanner. She had missed his level-headed clear thinking. He always helped her get her thoughts organized, so she could see what she had been missing.

"Could she be another dark magic plant?"

"Izzie isn't here anymore though, and they were after her."

Alison's gut clenched at the memories of the people who tried to take her friend away, and the lengths they had gone to try and harm her. She reminded herself that Izzie was capable and with her parents. She was likely having adventures and loving every moment.

"Well, what's to say that Christie isn't special like Izzie?" asked Alison.

"Or that it's not someone else after you. Brownstone seems to have put a stop to the Drow, but there could be other people who are after you. You're a Drow princess, that's very important to a lot of people."

Alison hated being reminded of that. She had no interest in taking up her place with the Drow.

"We need to speak to Christie and find out what her role in all of this is."

"Agreed."

CHAPTER TWENTY-FIVE

It was the big Louper tournament against one of the Cardinal's biggest rivals—the San Francisco Sandpipers. Emma looped her arm around Alison's glad to see her friend happier again. They made their way up the stands to where Kathleen and Peter had claimed some of the best seats. The crowd was buzzing as everyone was sure that the Cardinals would win this game and go on to the international tournament.

"They have this game in the bag. They kicked Sandpiper ass last year. They'll do it easily this year," Peter said, handing Alison a small bag of orange candies. "They're warming. It's cold out here."

Alison saw the gentle lick of orange magic within the thick candy shell and popped one into her mouth. The taste was an odd mixture of orange and clove, but the warmth soon spread through her stomach. The chill in the air faded away, making the situation much more comfortable. She was glad to be living in the world full of magic where life was a little easier.

"What is *that!?*" Kathleen gestured wildly at a black shape on the far side of the field.

A faint, red glow encompassed the silhouette giving it an even darker more dangerous appearance. She tried to figure out what it could possibly be. There was no denying that it wasn't friendly, but it wasn't making any attempt to get onto the field. It was simply standing there.

"I have no idea." Alison looked around to see if anyone else noticed it.

The shape was easily six feet tall. It seemed to be distorted as though halfway between man and beast. Everyone around them was laughing and talking about classes and the upcoming game. No one acknowledged the shape, or if they saw it, they didn't say anything about it.

"Is that Christie?" Kathleen pointed at a young blonde girl pushing her way down to the field.

Christie elbowed her way past the crowd as she desperately tried to get onto the field. People were growing increasingly hostile as the team walked out onto the field. She had to get there. She was so close. The Cardinals waved to the crowds, producing a roar of appreciation and excitement. This was going to be the game of the year. Everyone knew that the Cardinals would put on a good show, and they were almost guaranteed a spot in the big final.

Alison watched in horror as Christie ran out onto the field. She jumped from her seat and tried to get down to reach her. The smudge in her magic was growing as she watched. What if Christie was going to try and harm the team? Alison tried to push between a pair of elves and get down onto the field to stop Christie before she did something dangerous. She was racing across the field toward the silhouette. Tanner tried to use his larger size to clear a path for him and Alison, but Professor Regency stopped them dead in their tracks.

The gnome had forgone his usual glass of whiskey in favor of holding both hands up palms out toward the students. For such a small man, he had a very big presence, and he was using it to his advantage. Nothing was going to ruin that game. The team had trained hard, and they were up against one of their biggest rivals.

"No. The game starts in fifteen seconds," he said, blocking their way. "The spell has been cast already! Anyone on the field will be in the game. You can't go down there."

"That freshman is on the field. We need to get her back!" Alison tried to dodge around the gnome.

Max Regency was far more nimble on his feet than Alison had expected. He blocked her every move until the field vanished. Christie stood some twenty feet from the team, looking very confused as the broken tarmac of a long-abandoned road formed beneath her feet and scrubby bushes formed all around her. It dawned on her that she was stuck in the Louper game.

Everyone watched in horror as Christie became part of the most important game of the year. She looked around in confusion and panic. The team jogged across the tarmac and between the bushes to her. There wasn't time to ask her what on earth she thought she was doing. The Sandpipers would already be moving toward their goal. They needed to figure out a direction and start moving.

"What is this place?" Ethan gestured at the green and amber landscape around them.

"I don't know, but my instincts say we go that way." Luke pointed down what had been a road at one point.

"Keep up," the shifter said pointedly to Christie.

"Swipe her with a claw, just enough to wound her. It'll kick her out of the game," said Rex.

Christie's eyes grew wide and she drew back from Luke.

He growled low under his breath. "No, we don't play by those rules. We'll win the right way, without harming anyone." He levelled his gaze at Christie. "But you will have to keep up with us, understood?"

She nodded dumbly and tried to keep up as they jogged down the cracked and warped asphalt. She hadn't trained the way they had, and her physical fitness wasn't as good. Her breathing was labored as they approached an old wrought iron bridge. The railings curved up from the road with rusty struts holding them up. Luke wanted to be sympathetic to the girl, but they had worked far too hard to lose this because she had some crazy idea in her head.

They slowed down to allow Christie to catch her breath while Rex tested the viability of the bridge. He nudged it with his foot, and it stood sturdy. After a few good jabs and a long look for rust patches, they trusted it was safe and took off at a jog again. Trees grew up around them, and a thin mist rolled along the ground giving everything an eerie appearance. A chill ran down Christie's spine. This wasn't how it was supposed to happen.

The spectators watched as the team turned a corner and came across a long-abandoned church. Or at least they assumed it was a church. A small, dome-ceilinged structure sat on a concrete plinth with a large block of concrete at the front that looked suspiciously altar shaped. Slender boughed trees had burst up between the pillars and broken up the path that had once led up to the building.

"Do we look, or do we move on?" Ethan said, peering at it between the trees.

"Ethan and Rex, scout it out. We'll continue on." Luke gestured at his teammates before he picked up the jog again.

Christie was slowing them down. She wasn't complaining, but that didn't reduce Luke's frustration. Ethan and Rex caught up with after looking around the structure.

"Nothing, just an old crucifix."

"What do you think this place was?" Shannon asked.

"It's a ghost town," Christie said.

She'd read about them before moving to America. They didn't really exist in England, and she found them interesting. She had done some urbexing, or urban exploration, without her parents' knowledge of course. She and a couple of friends had gone out exploring abandoned buildings in their area. The old asylum was the creepiest. Christie would never forget the image of the small teddy bear sitting on the windowsill in one of the rooms. There was something heart breaking and shiver inducing about that teddy. It had been someone's once, and it sat there abandoned in a rotting room with peeling paint and the distinct sensation of silent screams.

Christie was right. The crowd saw the dilapidated buildings in the field on the other side of the shallow woods the team were jogging through. A wide road stretched out with crooked wooden buildings on either side. Dirty white curtains still hung in some of the windows as a reminder that it had once been someone's home.

The Sandpipers reached the town first, coming in at the opposite end. They paused in front of the old grocery store with the peeling blue paint on the warped wooden boards. Their captain peered into the large glass windows, looking at the neat rows of shelves. Some still had cans and jars on them. The previous owners had abandoned them to rot.

The Sandpipers went into the grocery store and quickly scouted around the shelves checking the jars, cupboards, and other little hidey-holes for some sort of a clue. There was something about the setting that made the captain think that maybe this was where they'd find puzzle pieces and keys to get to the gold disk. Satisfied that there was nothing there, they moved on. They needed to be systematic and efficient.

Christie needed to pause and catch her breath again. Luke restrained his wolf and the desire to snap at her. He was trying to give her the benefit of the doubt and assumed it was a dumb mistake that she was here.

"Check out that house there. I'll take Christie into the next one. We don't know what we're looking for exactly so use your experience." Luke pointed at the house next to them.

The greying, wooden boards were mostly straight and kept the building house-shaped. Thin yellow curtains hung in the rectangular windows. The small white picket fence around a patch of short yellowed grass really drove home how far the place had fallen. It must have been a family home at one point, full of love and laughter. Christie frowned, trying to focus. She was slowing the team down, and she hated that.

Luke moved the moment her breathing was down to an acceptable level. She followed him onto the rickety porch and through the plain wooden door inside. A thick layer of dust coated the wood floor and the peeling paint. The smell of dust and decay filled her nostrils and made her sneeze. Luke ignored her and started in the closest room, a small living room with over-stuffed couches now the home of rats. Thankfully the rats remained hidden in the darkness, and he was free to look around.

Christie had no idea what she was supposed to be looking for, but she went into the kitchen at the back of the house. Mugs and bowls were arranged on the table as though someone had made breakfast but never came down to eat it. The thick coat of dust showed that nothing had been through there in a good while. Lines were formed on the floor when she moved the chairs and opened the cupboards looking for who knew what.

The cupboards held plates and bowls, and there were a couple of cans with faded labels she couldn't read. They were sealed, so surely, they weren't what they were looking for? Granted she hadn't seen many Louper games, but those that she had, were nothing like this.

"I'll take the bathroom and master bedroom. You take the other bedrooms," Luke said from the doorway.

Christie cautiously followed him up the creaking stairs unsure where to put her hands or feet. She reflexively went to grasp onto the railing, but it crumbled beneath her hand when she tried. The next step sank deeper than she would have liked, and she rushed up the rest of them not wanting to fall through.

The bedrooms were simple with neatly made beds and old faded paintings that were now nothing more than rectangles of yellows and greys.

"Come on. We have a lot more buildings to check yet."

Luke led the way back out of the house. Part of him wished Christie had fallen through a rotten board or something, so she would be returned to the field and out of his hair.

"Nothing. Where to next, boss?" Ethan asked.

The shifter looked around the town, trying to be logical about this. There was no glint of the gold disk in the sunshine, and his instincts were oddly quiet. A familiar yipping call of coyotes filled the air, and his instincts kicked into full force. The coyotes had something they needed; he just knew it.

"Find those coyotes!"

Christie's mouth fell open. She was sure coyotes were nothing like Wyle E Coyote. If she remembered correctly, they bit—hard—and worked as an intelligent pack. Why were they heading toward them when they should have been running away?

The team listened intently for the direction of the coyotes. The Sandpipers emerged from a bar down the road and looked around for the coyotes. They had the same instinct. Luke glanced at Christie and really hoped she wasn't going to screw this up for them.

A group of ten or so canine forms slipped between two houses in the middle of the street. The crowd hushed when they saw the glint of silver around the neck of the lead coyote. It had a key.

Luke was the first one to spot the coyotes. His wolf side knew their scent all too well. He took off after the pack of grey and tan canines. They darted between bushes and scurried past fallen barrels before they took a sharp left and went into an old shop of some form.

Luke and a shifter from the Sandpipers were hot on their heels. They burst into the dust coated shop, listening intently for the sound of their claws clicking on the floor. Their scent was almost hidden beneath the dust and decay, but Luke picked it up. He leapt over barrels of something and ran into the back room where he saw a coyote's tail disappear out the back door.

The rest of his team circled the building, trying to cut off the coyotes, but Christie was slowing them down. While the team was fit and agile, she was struggling to traverse the terrain. The coyotes had moved into a space between four buildings. If the Cardinals were quick, they could cut off their escape route and get the key.

"Take the east corner, Dan. Rex and Shannon, take the west. Christie, the south," Ethan called.

Christie looked around trying to figure out what she was supposed to be doing. The others ran in their assigned directions and planted themselves between the buildings. Christie saw the last open gap, and the coyotes were running right for it. Their sharp teeth glinted, and she slowed her pace. What if they sank those teeth into her? Luke's expression of pure determination was focused on the silver key around the coyote's neck. Christie ran as fast as she could, but it wasn't enough.

The coyote shot through the gap between the buildings right into the waiting arms of the Sandpipers. The canine went oddly calm when the Sandpiper wizard wrapped his arms around it, and their captain plucked the key from its neck. The crowd groaned as they saw the Sandpipers take the clear lead. Now the Cardinals would have to follow behind them and try to use pure speed in the final race to the gold disk. Assuming that the key didn't just open a box to the disk.

"Why was that stupid freshman on the field in the first place?"

"Someone should have stopped her!"

"She screwed up the entire game!"

"Who is she anyway?"

Luke tried to tamp down his anger, but he saw the win slipping away, and it was Christie's fault. He had no idea what she was doing in the game, but he was going to chew her a new one the moment the game was done.

The Sandpipers watched as the key showed them a location. A drawer in the desk of what looked like the principal's office in the school. The crowd shouted the information to the Cardinals who of course couldn't hear. Ethan did manage to snatch a glance of it though. He wasn't sure about all the details, but he saw a drawer within a fancy desk.

"We need to find a fancy desk!"

"You're sure?" Luke dragged his fingers through his hair, feeling the defeat weighing on his shoulders.

"Yes! It was big and wooden, with some diploma thing behind it. It looked a lot like the headmistress's desk."

"The school!" Shannon blurted.

The Sandpipers were at the school already. They raced down the main hallway searching for the office. The Cardinals skidded around the corner and sprinted into the school. They saw as the Sandpipers enter the principal's office. They were halfway down the hall when the town vanished, leaving them in the field with a disappointed crowd.

Luke growled and swore. They should have won that game. They had the superior team. Fuck!

Christie quickly slunk away. The dark silhouette was gone, but she could feel his presence. The game was supposed to be the perfect distraction, and now she'd screwed everything up.

Alison and her friends rushed onto the field to offer comfort to the team. Luke was shaking his head and cursing.

"You were so close!"

"Thanks for the reminder," Luke growled and paced.

"Wasn't that your friend?" Ethan looked pointedly at Alison.

"I have no idea what she was doing! There was a dark silhouette on the far side of the field, and then she was running, and no one could stop her. Where is she now?" Alison looked around, trying to find Christie.

"Wait there was a dark silhouette? What if she's going to do her transfiguration spell right now?" Tanner gently clasped Alison's upper arms not wanting to worry her.

The silhouette had looked like something between man and beast. What if she had already started the spell?

"Dammit! We need to find her!"

Everyone turned and looked at Alison.

"You're the bounty hunter who can see magic trails," Kathleen said with her hands on her hips.

"Luke's the shifter with the nose to track her," Alison shot back.

There were no magic trails this time. No shining orbs to follow. It wasn't going to be that easy.

CHAPTER TWENTY-SIX

Christie kept her head down and remained close to the school building, ducking below the windows before she sprinted to the woods. He was waiting for her. She could feel it. Things hadn't gone very smoothly, but they were close now. They just needed one more small push, and she would be able to achieve her goal.

"She's clearly ashamed that she made the Cardinals lose their place in the finals. If I were her, I'd be hiding in my room, or somewhere safe," Kathleen said coolly.

Alison and her friends weren't the only ones looking for Christie. The professors and some other students wanted to ask her what on earth she thought she was doing. The Louper games brought the school together, and she had lost them a place in the final.

"We don't know which one is her room. She never told

us." Peter looked around for some freshmen. One of them had to know.

"Aren't you getting her scent or something, wolf boy?" Kathleen went to poke Luke.

Luke growled, causing her to step back. His patience was frayed, and Kathleen's pushing wasn't helping.

"Do you have any idea how many scents there are around here?" He took a step closer to Kathleen.

"She could be part of some dark magic. Alison and I think she's the book thief, and the books she stole point toward a dark and very dangerous ritual or spell," Tanner added, trying to think of a spell to track her down.

They had covered tracking spells but trying to find an individual student on the school grounds was difficult. There was so much magic there, and he didn't know Christie all that well. He'd have been able to find Alison or one of his friends easily.

"What sort of dark magic?" Kathleen turned to Tanner.

"A transformation from one magical type to another," Alison answered before she spotted someone she thought was a freshman.

"Hi, do you know Christie Beall?"

"Yeah, she's in the room next to mine, room eighty-nine."

"Thanks!" Alison gestured to her friends. They'd finally found her room.

"She's in room eighty-nine!"

They darted their way through the crowds heading back to the school for some warmth and comfort. The sun was beginning to set, and the temperature was plummeting. Their breath curled in white wisps as they crossed the grounds. The dragon flew above them, amusing himself by blowing puffs of icy air into various shapes from hearts to perfect circles.

The friends finally broke free from the crowd and bolted for the girls' dorms. The boys slowed, a bit unsure just how far they could go. It was one thing going to see their friends in the common room, but they still weren't allowed to step foot in the room, even if they'd bent the rules just that once. Alison grabbed Tanner's hand and tugged him in the direction of the room. She wanted him there. He was a part of this investigation, and he deserved to see it through to the end.

Kathleen hammered her fist on the door then twisted the handle and burst into the room. A trio of freshmen jumped up from their beds with their wands out. Christie wasn't in sight.

"Where's Christie Beall?" Alison demanded.

"We have no idea! What are you doing in our room?"

"Where would Christie go?"

The slender Light Elf pulled herself up a little taller and tried to look down her nose at the invaders. They had no right to be in her private space like that, and Christie had been kind to her.

"Why do you want to know?"

Alison and Tanner shared a look. If they were wrong, then spreading a rumor about Christie being involved in dark magic could ruin her reputation.

"She might be in trouble, and we want to help her."

The Light Elf looked back at her friends. They each wore expressions of deep distrust. Christie had been odd at first, but she had proven herself to be a good friend. They didn't want to give her up to these seniors who just barged into their room.

"She wanders down to the stream sometimes," the dark-haired witch finally shared.

Night time was fast approaching, and Alison didn't know how long they had before Christie continued with the dark magic. She couldn't help but remember the loss and destruction that occurred the last time dark magic had run rampant at the school.

Christie looked around the woods, trying to peer into the darkness and pick out his form. She could feel his presence, and a cold shiver sank into her bones and rooted her feet to the ground. A twig broke, and she spun around, trying to see who or what was nearby. Her heart raced, and she fumbled looking for her wand. She wouldn't be able to do much to him, not now, but she hoped she'd be able to give herself some time to run.

"You failed. Your friends will make fine sacrifices," a deep growling voice said from the darkness.

A flash of red caught her attention, and she saw his cold, predatory eyes staring at her. The scent of wet dog and moss filled her nostrils. He was closer than she'd thought. She wasn't going to let him hurt her friends. Pulling her wand, she tried to remember what professor Powell had taught her. All she needed was a simple fireball or something to drive him back so that she could run.

She swallowed her fear and tried to remember the words as her magic trickled into her wand. He stepped forward revealing a bare torso covered in muscle. His hands were tipped with sharp wolf claws, but his face was what made the words slip away from her.

What had once been a handsome man had been transformed into a monster. His jaw was caught between that of a wolf and a man, and sharp teeth were on display when he pulled back his thin, black lips. His short hair clung close to his skull and revealed pointed ears.

No. She wasn't going to be beaten like this. She lifted her wand and shouted the words before she turned and ran.

"There's something wrong in those woods. My pack and I caught a weird scent last time we ran together, but we couldn't find anything. It's back today, and my instincts say it's bad." Luke put his hand out to stop his friends where they stood.

They looked at the woods before them. The sun had set leaving only darkness between the familiar trees. They had walked through those woods many times over the years, and usually, there was a feeling of safety there. But tonight, goosebumps ran along their arms and the hairs on the back of their necks raised. Something was lurking in there, and their instincts were screaming at them to run.

Alison started to walk into the woods. She wasn't going to stand by and allow whatever darkness was there to hurt her friends. A crashing sound came from her left, and Christie burst out of the woods and raced toward the stables. Luke instinctively ran after her, his wolf side kicking in at the sight of potential prey running. The friends ran after him, wanting to talk to Christie and find out what was going on.

The younger girl stopped at the rise of a shallow hill and tried to catch her breath. Luke circled her, and his friends gathered around.

"What's going on, Christie?" Alison stood in front of her blocking her escape.

Christie raised her eyes to see the Drow's arms crossed and a look of anger on her pretty features.

"It's a long story, but we're not safe here. Not tonight," she said between gasps.

"We're not moving until you tell us what's going on, and why you took those books." Alison took a step closer.

"We can't stay here. Please. I'll tell you, just somewhere safe."

Dorvu saw the tension amongst the friends and landed near Alison, peering at the unfamiliar freshman.

"What's happening?" he asked.

"That's what we're trying to find out," Luke growled.

The dragon settled his wings and glared at the freshman, frosted air snorting out of his nose. He hated seeing his friends upset, and she seemed to be the cause of it.

Christie swallowed hard and risked a glance back at the woods. She could feel him there.

"My mum's really sick. She's dying. The healers don't know what's wrong with her or how to save her, but I found a way. There was a really old dusty book in the forbidden section of the magical library in London. If I can make this pendant, then I can save my mum. The problem is, I don't have enough magic to do it by myself. So, there was a guy; he seemed nice and friendly. He approached me when he saw me with the book." She paused to take a breath. "I don't know how he knew I had the book, but he did. I thought he was going to rat me out of the librarians, and they're really mean. They make the gnomes here look friendly. I've heard they cut off one poor boy's hand because he dared return a special book late."

"Get back to the point," Kathleen snapped.

Christie nodded and swallowed hard.

"He said that he could help me save my mum. He had this artifact that would give me the magic we needed because I didn't have any friends or anyone to help me. Dad was at mum's side all the time, and I'm pretty sure he forgot I existed. Anyway," she hesitated when she saw the expression on Luke's face and the sharpening of his teeth as he grew impatient. "He was a handsome shifter, but he didn't have a pack. He said he was tired of being treated like a mutt, a worthless beast. He said everyone looks down on shifters, and he wanted to become something more."

Luke stepped back and restrained himself from snarling. It wasn't the girl's fault. He was all too familiar with the prejudice against his kind, but he had a strong pack around him.

"We couldn't find the books he needed to make the transformation, but we found out that this school did. So, I managed to transfer to this school so I could get the books. I don't have the magic to steal the books by myself, and the gnomes guard them too well. So, he used an ancient artifact to unleash magic that he said would help me achieve our goals. It linked me to him, I think. I can feel him."

"Way to make it complicated," said Peter. "Not to mention dangerous. Artifacts are tricky at best and in the hands of a non-magical like a shifter, they can blow someone to pieces."

Christie went on, the words tumbling out, unheeded. "When I went to take the books, he took control of my body, and I went to... I don't know what it was. I think I was in the World in Between. I could touch the books, but I wasn't entirely in this world. It was the only way we could get the books. I can't lose my mum. I would do anything to keep her alive. I know it was stupid. The shifter used me like a puppet, but we were so close. He was going to help me make the pendant, and then everything would be okay."

Alison and Tanner looked at each other. Alison's sympathy for the girl was limited. She understood her desire to save her mother, but she had taken a ridiculous risk. Allowing herself to be used as a puppet sounded horrendous, and she must have known that such magic was dangerous.

"What went wrong?" Ethan asked softly and squeezed Christie's hand.

He had been in desperate situations, so he had more understanding of the girl's plight than the others. It was difficult knowing how far was too far when you were trying to save someone you loved.

"The artifact. It started to corrupt something within him so what little magic he had wasn't enough to finish the transformation. It pulled his wolf side out." Luke shivered at that image. "It stopped, and now he's stuck in this awful in between state and he needs help from a magical to fix it. He said he's going to sacrifice my friends unless someone helps him finish the transformation. He's insane! I feel so stupid for believing him and helping with this madness."

Ethan pulled the trembling girl gently into his arms and gave her a moment.

Luke was appalled at the idea of losing his wolf side, especially in such a horrific manner. Of course, he hated the way the magic community looked down on shifters, but he would never stoop to such darkness. He pitied the man who had felt the need to do so.

"Where is the artifact, Christie? What do you need for the pendant?" Alison asked, putting her hand on the girl's arm to try and focus her.

A mournful howl cut through the quiet of the night, and the dragon snorted. Luke's ears pricked, that wasn't one of his pack. It sounded wrong, distorted.

"I'm not exactly sure where the artifact is now. I'm not sure where it was. The shifter always took control, and I blacked out when I went to see it. I still need more magic to make the pendant. I have the herbs and stones; I just need more magic. He was supposed to help me once he became a wizard, but that's never going to happen now. I've completely screwed everything up, and you're not going to the Louper finals anymore. I'm really sorry."

"We'll deal with that later. We need to find and stop this deranged man first. Tell us everything you know, Christie." Alison tried to ground her in the moment.

Christie pulled herself together.

"His name is Scott. He was thrown out of his pack because of some disagreement with the alpha. All he wanted was to be respected, and he had kind brown eyes."

Alison's gaze hardened even as Christie was determined

to tell the rest.

"I'm not sure where he lived. It must have been somewhere nearby because the artifact's magic doesn't work if we're too far apart. I think it was in the woods on the edge of the grounds. The artifact is in an underground root cellar thing. It's got a low ceiling with thick roots going across it and lots of dirt and damp. We should tell Professor Powell. He deals with dark magic." She sucked in a deep breath of air.

"We don't have time for that. No, we can deal with this ourselves. By the time we've spoken to him and the others, who knows what this Scott will have done. You said he was looking for people to sacrifice…" Alison said.

A chill went through the students. It wasn't the first time they had faced down dark magic, but somehow this felt more dangerous. A twig snapped in the woods nearby, and a flash of darkness shot between the trees.

"Was that him?" Kathleen took a step closer to the woods.

"What are his weaknesses, Christie? What wizard magic does he have? We need more information on the artifact," Alison pushed.

The younger girl swallowed hard.

"He's still a shifter, and he doesn't have any magic of his own. The artifact is tied to darkness somehow. He said the shadows are the path to the gaps where he could transform."

"Does anyone have any ideas where this root cellar might be?" Alison looked around the group.

"No, but I might be able to track him." Luke allowed his wolf forward, making his eyes glint yellow.

"He's too dangerous. He wants us to go to him, so he can sacrifice us!" Christie argued.

"She has a point. It's not a good idea to play by his rules." Emma shifted her weight "I think we need to go directly to the artifact. That's his power, right?"

"Which direction, Luke?" Alison asked.

The shifter pointed toward the mountains. "It's not an easy hike. You'll need your night vision."

"I learned how to do that last week," Christie said glad to be of some use.

The older students gave her polite smiles. It was a simple spell they had learned in their freshman year too. You never knew when being able to see in the dark would get you out of trouble.

"I'll shift. My senses will be keener, and I can fight better in my wolf form," Luke explained as he began to transform.

Christie watched in awe. She'd never seen a shifter change before. Where once had been a tall, strong teenager now stood a powerful grey wolf. The wolf narrowed its eyes at her and yipped. The others were all casting their night vision spell, and once again, she was slowing them down. She pulled her wand and quickly whispered the words that allowed her to see through the woods almost as clearly as if it were day.

"I will watch from above," Dorvu announced, flapping his great wings.

There was a feeling of reassurance knowing the dragon would be close by. Alison had faith in her own magic, but with her friends' lives at stake, she would rather have more protection and defenses than less.

CHAPTER TWENTY-SEVEN

L uke led the way with Alison close behind. Tanner had entwined his fingers with hers to remind her that she wasn't alone. There was a determination in her eyes, and he didn't want her to feel as though she had to try and save everyone by herself.

Christie walked with Emma and Aya who were trying to reassure her.

"We'll fix this. Don't worry. We'll destroy the artifact and make the pendant, so you can save your mom." Emma squeezed Christie's hand.

Christie could feel Scott or the monster that he had become, lurking somewhere. There was a sense of him watching, but the bond had never been very good at locating him. It was something he used to control her, and she didn't know of a way to turn it to her benefit.

They made their way through the densely packed woods. A thick layer of fallen leaves covered the ground and hid small divots and branches that could twist your ankle. They had to walk slower than anyone wanted, the feeling of a ticking clock hung over them. The dragon flew overhead as close to the canopy as he could. Christie was sure Scott was in the woods with them somewhere, but she couldn't pinpoint where. She thought that he blamed her for the spell's failure and wanted to punish her. She wasn't going to allow him to harm her friends.

The trees grew more closely together, and the ground started to incline toward the foothills of the mountains. They had stepped through the boundary at the edge of the school grounds, and the security it provided. They were on their own now.

Silence filled the air. The usual sounds of owls hooting and insects chirping was entirely absent. Only the sound of their breathing and footsteps could be heard. Something was very wrong. Luke pushed forward with his ears up, listening for any sign of Scott. He thought he caught a weird scent of old moss and wet dog, but it came and went before he could track it. His hackles rose when he heard an unfamiliar footstep and the sensation of being stalked coursed through him.

Alison and her friends moved a little closer to Luke, closing the ranks and looking into the darkness for a predator. They hadn't realized they had done it, but Scott saw. A smile crossed his lips as he followed them from downwind where their shifter couldn't smell him. They were heading exactly where he wanted them to go. The ritual site was near the root cellar Christie had been trying to guide them to. He had cleansed it and prepared everything. All he needed was those students with their rich and potent magic. Soon. Soon, he would be the wizard he should have been.

The temperature dropped seemingly out of nowhere. Alison thrust her hands into her coat pockets and wished she'd brought her thick scarf. Tanner put his arm around her shoulders and held her close, trying to offer her a little extra warmth.

Ethan pulled warming candies from his pocket and passed them out without a word. They each took one and appreciated the added warmth. Luke stopped on top of a fallen log and bared his teeth. The area in front him felt wrong. Every instinct screamed at him to run away. Abominations lurked there.

Alison felt it too. A darkness that permeated the earth and filled the air with an unpleasant thickness. A bush rustled behind them, and Luke growled. Everyone spun around and saw him.

Scott stood over six feet tall with broad, strong shoulders and thick heavy muscle. His torso was bare and lightly covered with grey and tan fur. Long, black claws tipped his curved fingers, and his thin, black lips pulled back to reveal long white teeth. His once soft brown eyes were now a dark amber that glistened with malice and fury.

"A Drow will make a fine sacrifice." He walked closer to them.

The group stood strong not wanting to enter the dark clearing that felt so wrong. Ethan and Christie drew their wands while Luke slipped into the trees with plans of flanking the broken shifter.

"I'm afraid I don't have any room in my schedule for sacrifices." Alison smirked and carefully called on her magic. "Tonight has been blocked out for an ass-kicking."

Scott rolled his eyes.

"Stupid girl. You cannot defeat me. Save yourself some pain and anguish."

"I feel pretty good about this plan actually." Kathleen leveled her wand and formed an explosive spell in her mind.

A predatory grin spread across Scott's face as he felt the magic building in the girl's wand. She had plenty of magic for him to consume.

Brilliant white light filled the space between them as Kathleen fired the spell. It hit the center of Scott's chest, but it did nothing more than singe some of his fur. Kathleen swallowed hard, that should have blown him off his feet.

"You're going to have to try harder than that..."

"We need a plan," Ethan hissed.

Alison looked at the thick layer of magic that surrounded Scott. It sat in plates much like armor and was dark silver in color. She tried to find any chinks or weaknesses. Unlike physical armor, it didn't need gaps or such to allow for the wearer's joint movements.

He continued to advance on the students while she looked. There had to be a solution.

"Christie, you said the magic from the artifact was a shadow?"

"I think so." Christie stepped back.

"Hit him with light!" Alison commanded.

She was not going to be cowed by this monster. Stepping forward, she summoned all her magic and felt it filling her veins. Her friends called up every scrap of magic they could. No one was going to let this monster walk out of here.

Scott faltered. Light might, in fact, be able to harm him. He snarled and rushed Alison. Strong thighs tensed as his feet dug into the ground and propelled him forward at an alarming speed. His muscles bunched as he focused entirely on Alison. Fingers flexed, preparing to sink claws into soft, warm flesh.

The students worked as one. They released their combined magic as Scott leapt into the air, intending to slaughter Alison where she stood. Their magic collided with his body, and a blinding light exploded, knocking them all off their feet. Scott landed with a heavy thud on the ground where Alison had been. She struggled to right herself then rushed to Aya who was lying at an awkward angle next to the fallen log.

Luke didn't want to risk Scott getting back to his feet. He went for his throat intending to make sure his miserable life had come to an end. A strong hand wrapped around Luke's snout and tossed him bodily into a tree. The wind was knocked from his lungs and pain clouded his mind. Everything flickered black. He pulled on his internal strength refusing to be beaten that easily.

Aya was conscious again and pushed herself up into a sitting position. The dragon roared as he looked for a way down into the woods to help his friends. He flew as close as he could, breaking branches and sending them tumbling down onto the ground below. Ethan covered his head, trying to protect himself from the falling debris.

The dragon blew a blast of icy air at Scott, freezing him in place momentarily. It was enough for Alison to call her magic once more. There were cracks in the magical armor now. They were getting closer. Scott snarled and shook himself off, sending a shower of ice through the air. Luke got back onto his paws and lunged at Scott, sinking his teeth deep into the man's calf. His bite drew a furious shout from Scott before he started the death shake. His teeth tore through the muscle and tendons, filling his mouth with thick bitter blood.

Scott grabbed Luke's neck and threw him once more against the tree. His leg was in agonizing pain, but it was healing already. He still had enough shifter magic to heal at will.

Ethan, Alison, and Tanner all focused their magic on Scott once more. Kathleen watched over Aya while Emma ran to Luke's crumpled form.

The magic hit true once again, enveloping Scott in a brilliant white light. He clawed at it, desperately trying to remove the agonizing light that was tearing through his protections. The dark magic that had given him strength and power ebbed away as the light dissolved it. He wasn't done yet.

The students wavered. They could only maintain that level of constant magic for so long. Scott pushed forward fighting against the pain of the light. His claws were almost within reach of Alison's delicate throat when she dropped her magic and snatched up a broken shard of branch at her feet. Scott lunged for her. His claws raked her arm just before she drove the branch into his eye. He screamed in pain.

It was enough to ruin the other's focus, and the light magic stopped, giving Scott a chance to wrench the branch from his eye and start to heal. He glanced at the trees and contemplated running. Kathleen stepped away from Aya and began her own stream of light magic, striking him just over the heart. He moved to attack her, but Alison was right there. She picked up a larger branch and struck him in the side of the head.

The students rallied and stood as a united force with Alison the vision of a warrior, her shoulders back and magic flowing through her. Together they drove everything they had at Scott. Slowly, the dark magic disintegrated, leaving him exposed and vulnerable.

Alison dropped the branch and called her magic. Scott dropped to his knees, his torso a bloody, ragged mess. Alison engulfed him in her Drow magic, snuffing out his life and making sure that he would never sacrifice anyone.

Aya was on her feet again, and everyone rushed to Luke who was struggling to push himself up into a sitting position. His shifter healing had taken care of the worst of it, but he was still wobbly. He returned to his human form and leaned back against the tree while he waited for the spinning to stop.

"Team Awesome: one. Bad guy: nil," Luke said with a lopsided smile.

Everyone laughed. The rush of having won the fight buoying their spirits and staving off the exhaustion.

Luke coughed, and Ethan offered him a hand to help him stand.

"Now where were we on the whole saving your mom thing?"

Christie beamed at them all and threw her arms around Alison's neck. "Thank you!"

Alison gently hugged her back. "Where's this artifact? We need to destroy that and make your pendant."

"The weird door thing is just through here." Luke began walking toward the clearing.

The weight of the dark magic had vanished, and Dorvu swooped down eager to check that everyone was ok. Emma smiled and ran her hand over the dragon's large snout.

"We're ok, Dorvu."

The dragon still looked each of them over very carefully before he accepted that analysis.

"I will be close by."

With a flap of his wings, he returned to his position low in the sky to watch over them. Luke leaned on Ethan for the first few steps into the clearing while his healing took care of the rest of his injuries. He'd seen the door while running with the pack a few times, but they hadn't investigated. It wasn't shifter related, so they ignored it and carried on with their run.

"The artifact is some weird stone statuette made of the darkest black stone. He said it has something to do with shadow and the natural transformation from day to night and the between." Christie walked next to Alison, trying to seem as strong and confident as the older girl.

"So, we can destroy it with light." Kathleen looked at Alison. "I mean we destroyed his magic and that made him vulnerable to my blast of light."

Alison thought about it for a moment as they approached the door set into the ground. That certainly seemed sensible. Professor Powell would likely have preferred that they took the artifact to him to be studied, but she would feel better knowing that it was no longer in the world. If someone like Scott got their hands on it again, who knew what harm it could cause. Or worse, if the humans in town found it. They would have no idea how to control it.

Tanner reached down and pulled on the large metal ring on the door. To his surprise, it swung open easily. The hinges had been well-maintained. A set of stairs descended into the darkness. Tanner walked down cautiously, keeping his wand out, ready to defend himself against whatever nefarious things Scott might have left there.

The stench of death and wet dog filled the small space and Tanner covered his mouth. He formed a series of light orbs so they could see clearly. The night vision spell only worked when you had some form of light to work with, and it was pitch black down there. He regretted his decision as soon as he saw the remains of various animals stacked up in a neat pile behind a rustic altar.

Luke sniffed and snarled. "There are shifters among the dead."

"He must have been trying to get their help." Christie frowned "I had no idea."

"Let's get this over with," Kathleen said, striding over to the altar and pretending none of it bothered her.

They began looking through the small space for the statuette Christie had described. A small pile of rags had been put in the corner under a natural shelf formed in the earthen wall. A bed. It looked utterly miserable. Scraps of dried meat and old bones were stored in a bucket at the other end of the space. Books were strewn all around. Alison recognized their titles and frowned at their tattered state.

"He tore out relevant pieces and often took out his anger on them when they didn't have what he wanted." Christie picked up one of the books. "I tried to stop him."

"We'll worry about those later. Focus on finding the statuette." Alison looked through some of the wooden boxes. "Are you sure it'll be here?"

Christie poked a toe at his bed. "Yes. This was his sanctuary and where he felt the safest."

They systematically tore apart the cellar where Scott had lived for months. He had managed to pack a lot of stuff into the small space. They kept finding more books and notes frantically scribbled in an increasingly frantic hand. Small stores of old meat had been hidden behind boxes, rags, and in small holes in the walls.

Finally, Alison saw something within the altar. There was dark magic, just a small thread of it, but she was sure it was there.

"Help me move this." She gestured at the altar.

Tanner took one end of the hunk of wood, and Alison took the other. They slid it to the side and found a small, dark wooden box covered in dark magic. It had a faint hum to it that set everyone's teeth on edge.

Alison picked up the box. "We found it, or he has a second dark magic artifact."

She placed the box on the altar and inspected the magic. It appeared to be the same as what had wrapped around

Scott himself. The box was covered in a net of slate grey magic. When she ran her fingers over it, the grey magic shivered and moved away.

"Prepare your magic. We'll hit it with everything we have." Alison opened the box.

They focused as much light magic as they could summon on the small black statuette. It looked innocent to the naked eye. It was just a little man holding a large disk in his left hand. No human would have guessed at the amount of malevolent magic packed into such a tiny vessel.

Alison had to wonder why it had been made in the first place. Had the magic within it become corrupted? Was it something created by dark magic users for other dark magic users?

At first, it looked like their magic wasn't doing anything at all. The statuette swallowed up the light but didn't change in appearance. The friends were beginning to feel dismayed that their efforts weren't working. They didn't know what else to try. They hadn't studied how to destroy dark artifacts. Alison thought for a moment that perhaps she should start.

Just when they were ready to admit that the light magic plan failed, the statuette moved. Only a small fraction, but it definitely moved. Something was happening. Then it started to wobble and rattle around inside the box. The group was tired and wouldn't be able to keep up this level of magic for much longer. Their hands trembled as they maintained their focus.

This had to work. They couldn't leave the artifact there for someone else to stumble across and cause harm and damage. They weren't ready to give in just yet. The statuette's rattle increased in violence until it stilled entirely.

Suddenly the statuette exploded. Small black shards of stone flew through the air and disintegrated into dust when they struck the walls. The students hit the ground and covered their heads. They didn't have a moment to recover. The walls and the ground started shaking. Clods of earth fell from the ceiling and showered the students in dirt and grime.

"Out! Now!" Tanner shouted.

Aya and Emma scrambled to their feet and looked around making sure everyone was ok.

"Out!" Tanner gestured toward the stairs.

They couldn't afford to stand around when the entire room was crumbling around them. Roots loosened from the packed dirt and fell into the shrinking space. The floor was covered in fallen debris which made moving more difficult. They tried to run to the stairs, but the steps were slowly being buried, and the exit was growing smaller by the second.

Emma summoned her magic. She looked at the exit and forced herself to speak the words to move the dirt aside. The fresh earth exploded outward, causing the dragon to cry out in alarm. Emma pushed Aya and Christie up the stairs and out into the cold night.

Alison jumped over the altar and grabbed the back of Luke's shirt as he struggled to get his leg out from under a large lump of dirt.

"Come on. You're a shifter! Use that fabled shifter strength!"

Luke pulled harder on his leg. Alison yanked on his

shirt, and the added momentum broke Luke free, allowing him to run.

Tanner weaved magic to support the stairs, so they didn't collapse before everyone was out. Kathleen shot past him. Alison and Luke were almost there. Tanner shoved Ethan up the stairs. He wasn't going to move until all his friends were safely out.

Alison and Luke crowded up the stairs as the room continued to shake and fell apart around them. Alison grabbed onto Tanner's hand and wrenched him along with her. She wasn't about to risk him being buried alive down there.

They scrambled out into the clearing and stumbled a few steps before the room collapsed completely, leaving a pit in the ground. They fought to catch their breath, then Ethan laughed.

"Well, that was an adventure!"

They had to laugh along with him.

"The multi-dimensional classes have paid off." Tanner laughed, trying to wipe the worst of the dirt off. "Professor Wilson would be proud of us."

"Oh, I'm sure he'd have some scathing comment." Alison tried to get a piece of root out of her hair. "He usually has something to add about our methods."

"We got out alive. That's good enough for me."

Everyone agreed.

CHAPTER TWENTY-EIGHT

"We need the books to make the pendant!"
Christie got down onto her hands and knees and started to dig in the loose soil, trying to find the books. Kathleen sighed and leaned back against the tree. The books could stay down there for all she cared. She'd had quite enough dirt and trouble for one evening.

"Stand back." Aya stood. "I convinced Librarian Decker to teach me the spell they use to retrieve late books."

"When!?" Emma looked at her friend surprised.

"A few months ago. It sounded handy for when I lost books around the house." Aya shrugged.

Christie moved back and watched Aya warily. Aya calmed herself and remembered the smooth motion the gnome had taught her.

She gave a flick and a slow sweeping motion of her wand. The ground started shifting, and to everyone's delight, the books all flew toward Aya then stacked themselves neatly at her feet.

"I suppose this means we're making a pendant." Kathleen pushed herself off the tree. "What are we going to need?"

Christie ran to an old oak tree and retrieved a cream tote bag.

"I have everything in here. I just need more magic to help me pull it all together."

She emptied the contents of the tote onto the ground and arranged it in an order that made sense to her. A trio of clear crystals sat next to a collection of dried herbs, and translucent ribbons were bundled around a delicate glass bottle.

"This will save my mum. It's an ancient healing charm."

Alison looked down at the items. "And you're sure it's not another dark magic spell. Absolutely sure?"

"As sure as I can be."

Emma walked over. "What do we need to do?"

They were all exhausted, but they couldn't leave the girl like this. She had screwed up big time, but she was doing it with the best of intents.

"The crystals will hold the magic and become the pendant. We need to say these words while we crush the herbs and add them into the potion. Then we have to speak these words while we tie the ribbons around the potion. Then finally we'll pour the potion on the crystals, and they'll become the pendant. I think it'll take about an hour. The words are a bit of a tongue twister. I don't even know what language they're in."

Christie held out the spells they needed. Alison looked at them. The language wasn't something she recognized, but her magic did. The words formed on her tongue with the same ease that English did. She handed them to Kathleen.

"And you're sure it's as simple as that?" Kathleen looked at Christie. It felt a bit too easy.

"Yes. I put a lot of research into this. It took me months to track down those herbs, and another month to make the potion. The ingredients are very rare. I had to ship some of them from Tibet."

Everyone formed a loose circle and stood where they could all see the words of the spells.

"Ready when you are." Tanner smiled down at Christie.

Christie had memorized the words already. They brought her comfort during the darkness, the knowledge that she was going to save her mum.

She began crushing the herbs while they all said the first part of the spell. The magic thrummed, and Alison watched as the herbs turned a bright pink where the magic was released and transformed. No one said a word not wanting to ruin the spell. They watched in silence as Christie carefully added the crushed herbs into the potion. The potion bubbled and hissed, turning a sky blue. Threads of gold magic wove through it to Alison's vision, and she smiled. There were no signs of dark magic yet.

They continued through the spell careful to enunciate the words while Christie focused on completing the motions perfectly. When the crystals came together to form a large garnet colored stone, something changed. Alison saw a darkness rise from the crystal. A malevolent force with an indiscernible shape. The magic was pure black; darker than anything she had seen before. It was far more evil than anything they'd encountered. She watched as it vanished into the woods while everyone else focused on the pendant.

The pendant settled into a pretty pale amethyst color full of gold sparkles of positive healing magic. Christie grinned and gripped it in her hand tightly.

Everyone looked at Alison.

"I can see the healing magic in it." She smiled and decided not to say anything about the darkness. Not yet.

Christie stood and smiled shyly.

"Thank you. All of you. I can't tell you how much this means to me. I've been terrified that I'll lose my mum, and I really can't lose her."

Emma squeezed her hand. "It's what friends are for."

"We get it. I'm sure we'd do whatever it took to save each other's lives, too." Tanner smiled at Christie. "Just talk to someone next time. You're not in this alone."

"We should return those books to the gnomes. It's been killing them having books missing from their library." Ethan bent down to pick up some of the books. "You'd have thought they were treasure."

"If we leave them near the kitchen door, then someone will find them, and Christie won't get into trouble." Emma smiled at Christie. "She was doing it for good reasons."

"They're going to be furious when they see the state of some of these books." Tanner brushed the dirt off a particularly old looking tome.

"I'm sure they'll be talking about it for years." Kathleen picked up an armful of books. "They'll feel better having something to gripe about. Something other than late fees that is."

"The gnomes really aren't that bad," Aya said, picking

up the last of the books. "They care about the books because they hold knowledge. That's important for the world as a whole."

Kathleen rolled her eyes. "When did you get all philosophical?"

"You know that knowledge lets you wear that make-up and gives you the expensive magical items you love so much, right?"

Everyone's patience was frayed, and Aya wasn't in the mood for Kathleen's commentary and attitude. She knew that her friend meant well, but knowledge was important. It was the bedrock of society and making snide comments about it didn't help anyone or anything.

They began the slow walk back through the woods toward the school. The dragon remained close, following behind them in case something should try and harm them. He was a little disappointed that he hadn't been able to do more to save the day. Once they were out in the open space of the fields again, he went looking for rabbits to turn into popsicles.

"Next time something happens, talk to your friends first." Alison looked at Christie. "I promise it's a better option than trying dark magic."

"Especially once Alison's a bounty hunter." Luke nudged Alison playfully. "No one will go near dark magic when there's a threat of her hunting them down."

"I think it's so cool that you're going to be a bounty hunter! You're following in your dad's footsteps, right? My dad does some boring office job. It has something to do with cataloguing magic items and registering wands. I think. I didn't really listen because it sounded boring, and I want to do something amazing. I don't think I could be a bounty hunter, but maybe I'll be an archaeologist, digging up awesome old artifacts!"

"I've had enough of artifacts," Peter said, shifting the weight of the books to be more comfortable. "I'll be quite happy if I never see another one. Ever again."

"Are you telling me you didn't have fun battling the forces of evil?" Tanner looked at him.

"I'd much rather report on evil than actually fight it. I can help keep people safe through the spread of important information. Leave the ass-kicking to Alison."

"Is that what you've decided on? Journalism?"

"Yeah, I think so. I can make a difference. Words are powerful, and the world needs honest journalists who bring the news to the people. Propaganda can win or lose a war, and the truth can too."

Horace watched the group walking across the grass as though nothing had happened. He didn't miss the books in their arms. The students were all there at the school to be trained to protect and help the world. They were the first line of defense in a dangerous world full of magic. That particular group of students was something else though. They weren't just going to protect the world—they were going to change it.

"I told 'em that girl was trouble," Estelle said, blowing a smoke ring.

Estelle had tried to warn Alison in her own way. She had seen Christie sneaking into the woods, and that corrupted shifter hadn't escaped her notice either. Nothing got past Estelle.

"Her heart was in the right place. She just needed her friends around her."

"Those kids could have been killed. And don't think I didn't notice that darkness that shot out of the woods earlier."

Horace frowned. He hadn't missed that, and he doubted Alison had either. There were always consequences to the type of magic they'd performed in the woods. That pendant was made with the intent of saving a life, but everything must balance. A darkness emerged into the world to balance the life that would be saved. There was nothing much to be done about it at that moment. Who knew where the darkness had gone, or even what exactly it was. He might have a quiet word with Mara and Xander about it, without mentioning the students.

"That Christie girl isn't all sweetness and light, you know." She took another drag of the cigarette dangling between her lips. "She likes to bend the rules a little too much. This won't be the last of the trouble she causes."

"I know, Aunt Estelle, I know. She has good people around her now though. Her path has become a bit clearer tonight."

"Let's hope she sees that for herself and makes the right decisions. She's on the cusp that one; she could go either way."

The students snuck around the back of the school, ducking beneath the windows so as not to be seen. If they got caught with the books in their arms, there would be a lot of explaining to do. The punishments for dealing with Scott and stealing the books, let alone making the pendant using a forbidden spell would be very steep. They carefully placed the books down outside the door where someone was sure to stumble over them. Once that was done, they returned to the school as if nothing had happened.

"Do you think they'll take pity on us and let us eat dinner late?" Ethan asked, his stomach growling.

"There's one way to find out," Emma said, putting her arm through his.

"It would be a crime to let us go without food," Kathleen pouted. "I'm sure of it."

"Missing one meal won't kill you," Tanner said, rolling his eyes.

They made their way to the dining hall and found it almost empty. The pixies bustled around cleaning up the crumbs and glaring at the remaining few students still eating. The friends sat at the closest table where they hoped the food would form in front of them as it usually did.

To their relief, a generous helping of meatloaf with mashed potato soon appeared. Luke dug in the moment immediately. He was absolutely ravenous. Healing like he had really taken it out of him. The pixies sighed and shook their heads. These students really had no manners at all.

CHAPTER TWENTY-NINE

It was the last day of term, and the feeling was bittersweet. Alison and her friends had gathered up all the gifts they had bought and hidden from each other. Kathleen insisted on trying to see which ones were for her, so she could guess. No one indulged her, and she was made to wait until after the traditional Christmas dinner.

"It won't kill you to wait another hour." Emma held the bag full of gifts a little closer. "You're acting like a toddler."

The seniors had spent most of the morning decorating the hall, as was the tradition. There had been some arguments over how exactly to do it, but Alison thought it had come together beautifully. The younger students entered into the hall first, and a flush of happiness filled the girls when they saw the joy and awe on the students' faces.

They had decided to go with a traditional theme. Gold and red with small splashes of natural holly leaf green. Alison had personally formed and hung each of the hundreds of small, red glass baubles from the ceiling. Every one of them was unique with a slightly different pattern and decoration. The magic had been intricate, but she loved how it had come together. Kathleen had insisted on doing the thick, fluffy gold tinsel that draped from the corners and around the edges.

Natural holly and ivy wreaths were hung at even intervals on the walls. They had taken some of the students a long time to coax the inherent magic within the plants to bend to their will. The wreaths were all perfectly round and added a little elegance and class to the whole thing.

Each table had its own unique centerpiece, with the largest and most extravagant belonging to the professors' table. Their centerpiece had required a convoluted spell to bring together the natural holly, pine cones, and mistletoe with the magically formed glass works and candles. Glass reindeer cavorted with cheerful Christmas elves, and small brightly colored presents nestled between the leaves.

Alison and her friends headed over to the large table Emma and Aya had decorated. The white tablecloth featured red snowflakes. The centerpiece was an elegantly twisting formation of small red and gold baubles. Each bauble had one of the friends' names written on it in snow white ink, a personal touch that Alison appreciated.

She hoped Izzie was enjoying a nice meal somewhere. Izzie had always enjoyed the big Christmas meal. It was impossible not to be happy when you were surrounded by such joy. She looked at her friends, at the broad smiles, and the warm glow of contentment in their souls and she allowed herself to revel in it. She couldn't ask for better company.

The Christmas feast appeared as the friends sat down and tucked their bags of gifts beneath their seats. A warm chestnut soup filled the white bowl and permeated the air with the rich aroma that made Alison's mouth water. She took a spoonful and found it to be even better than she had expected.

"I wouldn't have thought you could make soup from chestnuts, but this is really good," Ethan said between spoonfuls.

"It sounds ridiculous, but I wouldn't say no to more." Kathleen dabbed her mouth with her napkin. "Although, I am looking forward to the main course."

"I'm not a big fan of turkey. I hope there's plenty of roasted potatoes this time." Luke finished his soup. "The potatoes are the best part."

"Blasphemy!" Peter looked aghast. "The pigs in blankets are the best part!"

Luke raised his eyebrow.

"I'll trade you some of my pigs in blankets for some of your roasted potatoes…"

"An equal trade. You're not getting my roasted potatoes for one measly pig in a blanket."

Luke grinned. "I would never."

"You boys take food so seriously." Kathleen placed her napkin down. "You'd have thought you both were wolves."

Luke ignored the jibe and looked at the full holiday dinner that had formed on the plate in front of him. The turkey was perfectly cooked, and the helping of cranberry jelly was very generous. As he had expected, they had skimped on the roasted potatoes though.

"I'll give you three pigs in blankets for those potatoes." He gestured at three of the potatoes on Peter's plate.

"You can have two of those potatoes."

Luke looked down at his plate and back at Peter's. He passed over the pigs in blankets and devoured the potatoes before anyone could think about taking them from him.

Dessert was a trio of puddings. The first was a decadent chocolate pudding covered in a thick layer of fudge. The second was a light lemon tart that melted on the tongue, and the final was a creamy, rich toffee roulade. The friends leaned back in their chairs feeling almost too full to move.

Once the plates disappeared, Alison picked up her bag of gifts.

"Shall I go first?"

"Do me first. I'm dying to see what you got me!" Kathleen beamed.

"This is from all of us." Alison pulled out the small box from her bag.

It had been difficult to wrap it in the thin silver silk. The box was so small that it had required some magical assistance to make it look neat.

Kathleen inspected the box and pursed her lips.

"Well, given the size, it has to be a crystal or jewelry."

She carefully unwrapped it, keeping the silk flat and undamaged. Her eyes widened when she opened the box and saw the earrings nestled inside.

"We thought they would go with any outfit." Alison reached across and touched her friend's arm. "They're a rare dwarven gem."

"They're the most beautiful thing I've ever laid eyes on." Kathleen swiped at her eyes. "Thank you all so much!"

She pulled Emma and Peter into a hug; they were the closest to her.

Christie approached with a small bag of her own and a smile on her face.

"Hey, I got you guys some gifts. Do you mind if I give them to you? Oh, Kathleen, you got your earrings! Do you like them?"

"You chipped in, too?"

"We wanted to get you something really special."

Kathleen couldn't take her eyes off the delicate roses. They meant more to her than she could express.

"We got you something, Christie." Aya retrieved a slender envelope from her bag.

"This is from everyone."

Christie opened the envelope, and her jaw dropped.

"They're my favorite band ever, and I've never been able to see them in concert! How did you get tickets? They're almost impossible to get!"

"We have our methods." Aya smiled. "I'm glad you like them."

"They're amazing, thank you so much! Oh, I got you something, too."

Christie handed Aya a gold wrapped present with a sapphire blue ribbon neatly tied around it. Aya opened it to reveal a candle that will burn for a year and change scents depending on what the owner needed at that moment. It would smell of warm cookies and open fire when they needed comfort, or an open meadow when they needed to feel calm freedom.

"This is wonderful. Thank you so much, Christie. It's very thoughtful."

Christie handed out a few more gifts before she said

her goodbyes and returned to her own table. She was finally making friends with girls in her dorm and year.

Tanner handed Alison two boxes. She set down the simple long box wrapped in brown paper and opened the first one. Inside was the book, The Tales of Arashi. "You remembered!" She ran her hands over the cover.

"I get it," he said, "sometimes the past brings back only good memories."

She kissed him on the cheek, her eyes shining and picked up the second box.

Alison opened it to reveal a beautiful knife with a simple black hilt and a dark purple stone in the guard.

"I also wanted you to know, I believe in you. You can store some of your magic in it. So, when you're a bad ass bounty hunter, you'll have a knife to help you in a fight. And if somehow you can't access your full magic, you'll have a small store in the knife. Only you can access the magic."

Alison wrapped her arms around Tanner's shoulders and hugged him tightly. She was overcome by how sweet and thoughtful the gift was. "I'm not happy about losing you for a year to the bounty hunting gig, but I still support your decision."

"I can't tell you how much that means to me."

They continued to exchange gifts and enjoy the warm bubbly atmosphere of the afternoon. Everyone was happy with what they had received. The time came to say goodbye for the holidays and head back home.

The girls returned to their room where they carefully stowed away their new gifts. Alison looked around the room one last time. This was the last Christmas she would spend here, and it was an odd feeling. The sky wore a thick, pale grey coat of low hanging clouds. Alison sighed in contentment, feeling like she was ready to move on.

"It looks like snow." Emma pointed out the window.

The dragon swooped down in front of their window and started blowing great heavy gusts. Alison wasn't sure if it was going to snow naturally, but the dragon formed snow of his own. Large flakes fell from where the dragon had blown his ice magic. The clouds soon started adding their own snow, and the girls couldn't help but feel ecstatic. It was the perfect ending to the Christmas afternoon.

The green grass was soon covered in a velvety layer of crisp white snow. It was a winter wonderland. Alison and her friends bundled up in thick scarves and gloves with added magic to keep them warm and toasty.

Emma pulled Alison close. "Have the most amazing Christmas holiday. I look forward to seeing you next year. Isn't it weird saying next year!?"

They hugged and wished each other happy holidays full of good food, laughter, and joy before they slowly filed out of the room and went to meet the boys. Tanner took Alison to the side and kissed her softly.

"I'm going to miss you."

"I'll miss you, too." Alison leaned against him.

She was looking forward to seeing Brownstone and Shay again, but that didn't remove the fact she hated being away from Tanner for long stretches.

Tanner stroked her cheek. "Don't get into or cause too much trouble!"

"I'll leave that to Shay." Alison grinned.

"I'll see you next year." Tanner turned, picked up his bag and walked out into the snow.

Alison said her goodbyes to Luke and told him to pass on her best to his pack. Then she was ready to head out to the jitney herself. It had been an interesting year, and she felt as though she was one step closer to achieving her bounty hunter dreams.

A flicker of shadow moved in the corner of her eye. She turned and swore she saw something not entirely of this world on the horizon. A coldness filled her stomach, and she remembered the darkness that had emerged from the pendant. She'd been so happy to help save Christie's mom that she'd forgotten about it entirely.

"Come on, Miss Brownstone. Some of us would like to get home before Christmas next year!" Mrs. Beasley called.

Alison picked up her pace and climbed onto the jitney. Mrs. Beasley had decorated the small bus with red and gold tinsel and emerald colored ribbons. She ducked beneath a particularly low-hanging piece of tinsel and wove around stray bags in the aisle as she looked for a seat. Spirits were high, and some students had formed small ethereal reindeer and sent them racing through the air.

Mrs. Beasley shook her finger at them, still smiling. "Not on the jitney." The reindeer leaped over a seat and disappeared into the air.

Soft bells jingled from somewhere before a snowball collided with Mrs. Beasley's red Santa hat.

She levelled a glare at the junior who had dared form a snowball let alone thrown it on her jitney. The student cowered.

"If anyone else so much as thinks about throwing a

snowball on this bus, I'll leave you stranded in the middle of nowhere, and you can try and walk home."

Silence descended on the bus, and Alison finally found a seat next to a sophomore she'd seen in the corridors. The quiet witch looked out the window lost in her own thoughts, and Alison was grateful for it.

"Did you hear the books showed back up?"

"I heard the gnomes were furious, and some of them had pages missing!"

"Didn't they put a bounty out for whoever had damaged the books?"

"They tried, but no one would take it seriously. The last I heard they're trying to form new spells to protect the books and punish students who don't look after them."

Alison felt a little bad for the gnomes. They threw their strong protective instincts into guarding those books, and they were irreplaceable. She knew one of them had come from Professor Powell's own personal collection, but he hadn't said a word about it. She didn't want to be on his bad side, so she hoped he never found out about her involvement in the entire situation.

The ride back to the Starbucks was riotous. A freshman started singing Rudolph the red-nosed reindeer, and it descended into mayhem from there. The ethereal reindeer were joined by what Alison thought were Santas in sleighs. They raced around the jitney using the tinsel and ribbons as an assault course to be navigated at the highest speeds. One of the sleighs missed the turn and crashed into the window, leaving a small white snowflake on the window.

Mrs. Beasley put on some Christmas songs and turned the volume up high. Everyone sang along at the top of their voices, and Alison found herself joining in. The joy and happiness were infectious.

Alison was the last person to get off the jitney. She was eager to see Shay and Brownstone again but trying to get through the crush of bodies just wasn't worth that extra couple of minutes. The train would arrive at the same time regardless.

"Have a great Christmas, Mrs. Beasley," Alison said brightly.

"Oh, I will. I have some very nice chocolates with my name on them."

Alison walked into the bustling Starbucks full of laughter and the traditional scents of Christmas. Cinnamon, nutmeg, and spun sugar seemed to fill the air. The usual acoustic music had been replaced with Holiday songs.

People were crowded around the front counter, and it took Alison a few minutes to weave her way between the tables full of humans and get to the wall by the bathroom. She glanced back for a moment and wondered what it would be like to be a normal human. To be entirely oblivious to what had happened at the school over the past few days.

She didn't envy them, but her desire to protect them was growing. Alison went through the back wall and made her way down the twisting stairways to her platform. The railway would take a magical from where they were to anywhere in the world. That made the path from one platform to the next a very complicated business. Fortunately, the signs were mostly clear, and she hadn't gotten lost in a good while.

A feeling of hope filled her chest as she thought about seeing Shay and Brownstone again. Christmas was a time of celebration and family. They were the perfect family for her. Alison stepped onto her platform and joined the ranks of other magicals likely heading home for the holidays. The familiar bright red train soon appeared in a small puff of steam. Alison patiently waited for the passengers to disembark before she got on and looked for a seat. She was going home, and nothing could remove the feeling of happiness that thought brought her.

That was until she saw the flicker of darkness out of the corner of her eye. She turned to see the ambiguous shadow lurking at the very edge of the platform, far from any other commuters. It could have been an oddly shaped shadow cast by the magical lights over the platform. It could have been, but Alison knew differently.

The End

Alison returns in her last adventure at the School of Necessary Magic in Epic Is Her Future.

Don't miss the thrilling conclusion.

Secrets are revealed. Enemies are vanquished. Lives are changed forever.

What's funnier than a swearing, troublemaking troll?

A trick or treating swearing, troublemaking troll.

Sign-up and keep up to date with all things Oriceran and receive a free copy of Trick or Troll, a short story starring YTT. (Other people are in it, too.)

GET IT NOW!

It's a Saturday afternoon in the new house and there's a team of people working diligently to fix a few things. Tip if you're buying a new house – there will be a lot to fix at first.

They're whispering to each other in hushed tones, (I'm assuming because here I sit working on author notes) and keep calling me ma'am, or worse, Miss Martha. Takes me back to the days when I was a small child in rural Virginia and my dad was the minister at a small Episcopal church in Washington, Virginia. All his parishioners called me, Miss Martha and there was a certain amount of respect given, just because dad was the preacher, even to a smartalecky kid, which I have been from the moment I was born. My goal is to raise it to the level of art form or ridiculousness – whichever is fine with me.

Ridiculousness is winning and if that's who I am, that's a good thing. I'm on the crest of turning 60 (one year to go), and finally figured out it's better to find my tribe. The ones who like a girl who dreams up magic places, swears a bit (perhaps quite a bit), likes to run, draw cartoons, invite people over for dinner (the Offspring once put one of those invites on FB and I just went with it – it was a great time in a tiny kitchen), doesn't eat meat (yes, it's true – I got a dog with a sweet face who's smart, and that led to this thought that kept creeping in every time I made a burger that just days ago, this was a frightened cow – I couldn't do it anymore), loves to write, can't eat gluten without keeling over (but knows that there's no gluten in whiskey), gets a library card first thing when I move (and once used it as an ID to get into a secure building in Chicago), fascinated by the weird things people create (like the lady who covered her house in colorful bits of metal), and believes that good will find me in the end.

I've stood out from the beginning, but wanted to fit in, blend in to the background. Life had other plans. To start off I was 5'9 at the age of 11 with wild, curly blond hair. I was taller than some of my teachers and looked like a stick with a pompom on top.

And, for as long as I can remember someone has told me that I'm 'opinionated', which by the way translates to 'not the same opinion as mine'. When I was younger, and if a cute boy was involved, I tried to keep quiet and get along. But eventually, I let loose and said what I was really thinking. Picture shock on cute boy's face and relief on mine. It never worked out.

If I had it to do over again, I'd be myself and let those who want to walk away, get to gettin'. Eventually, I would have found my people because eventually I have and have invited them in. Weird, interesting, creative, passionate, kind people with something to say and a boundless curiosity in the world mixed with a snarky sense of humor and a nice dash of belief in the goodness of others. Very important to me.

That brings me to the last thought on this Saturday morning (team has left, and house is quiet for the moment). It's never too late to go back to the factory settings and bring out that kid, more and more and celebrate her – let her lead. That's my goal for whatever years I have left. Be myself more and more and see where it leads. More adventures to follow.

THANK YOU for not only reading this story, but these author notes as well .

When Martha and I conceived of the concept for the School of Necessary Magic, I knew that I was a little in trouble.

Why?

I'm glad you asked.

You see, I didn't know the YA market that well. The emotions that often go into a YA focused book are not the same ones that I usually enjoy reading, so I told her flat out, "You got this, right?"

Martha swore up and down she did, so we went ahead and made the series happen.

We really appreciate the support you have shown us with reading this series, and the troubles and travails of our teenage antagonist, Alison Brownstone.

Now, whether Martha has done this or not, I'm going to talk about the next SoNM (School of Necessary Magic) series we are looking to do.

When Martha and I were talking last week on this subject, and what is next for the school, we looked at the various characters we had created and wanted something different. As we usually do, we 'discussed' the options and finally decided that we wanted to come at the story from a different direction.

We chose to come at the story with a mundane with a witch's powers.

'BUT WAIT!' you say? We can't have a mundane with witch's powers in Oriceran you argue, and you would be right. We can't.

But rather, our protagonist has been raised with a mundane for a father, one who wasn't sure if she would ever have powers, and chose to raise her as regular as he could. Not because he is against Oricerans, but rather with his love for his daughter he could only raise her with what he knows.

And he knows how to be a mundane.

When a representative from a Government agency knocks on his door late one afternoon, with his daughter next to him as he opens the door he gets a rather startling surprise.

His adopted daughter has just wiped out three bullies and not with the martial arts she has been taught.

But with magic she was never taught to wield.

When he invites the agent in with his daughter, they both learn about a special school from the agent. One where those who have magic can be taught and supervised, protected from those who would wish to use the talents and abilities for nefarious purposes and grow in their powers.

And so, I'd like to inform you that there is another series in the School of Necessary Magic stories on the horizon.

The Determined Witch - Coming to you winter 2018/2019.

You can never keep a determined witch down.

#TooWitchyForYou

Ad Aeternitatem,

Michael Anderle

OTHER SERIES IN THE ORICERAN
UNIVERSE:

SCHOOL OF NECESSARY MAGIC
THE DANIEL CODEX SERIES
I FEAR NO EVIL
THE UNBELIEVABLE MR. BROWNSTONE
THE LEIRA CHRONICLES
REWRITING JUSTICE
THE KACY CHRONICLES
MIDWEST MAGIC CHRONICLES
SOUL STONE MAGE
THE FAIRHAVEN CHRONICLES

BOOKS BY MICHAEL ANDERLE

For a complete list of books by Michael Anderle, please visit

www.lmbpn.com/ma-books/

All LMBPN Audiobooks are Available at Audible.com and iTunes. For a complete list of audiobooks visit:

www.lmbpn.com/audible